H9-13

Guns in Wyoming

Center Point
Large Print

Also by Lauran Paine and available from
Center Point Large Print:

The Guns of Parral
The Man Without a Gun
Beyond Fort Mims
Ute Peak Country
Way of the Outlaw
The Plains of Laramie

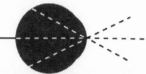

**This Large Print Book carries the
Seal of Approval of N.A.V.H.**

Guns in Wyoming

Lauran Paine

Center Point Large Print
Thorndike, Maine

A Circle Ⓥ Western published by
Center Point Large Print in 2013 in co-operation with
Golden West Literary Agency.

First Edition, June 2013.

Printed in the United States of America
on permanent paper.
Set in 16-point Times New Roman type.

ISBN: 978-1-61173-746-2

Library of Congress Cataloging-in-Publication Data

Paine, Lauran.
  Guns in Wyoming / Lauran Paine. — First edition.
  pages cm
  ISBN 978-1-61173-746-2 (Library Binding : alk. paper)
  1. Wyoming—Fiction. 2. Large type books. I. Title.
  PS3566.A34G8478 2013
  813′.54—dc23
                                             2013006495

Chapter One

There was a host of warm stars around a clear moon and the night was fragrant with soft spring air. That was the night they did it: May 20th, 1885.

There were three cowboys riding down from the sheep camp at Shipman's Meadows, liquid dark shadows moving through a lovely night, one behind the other saying nothing, swaying with their saddles, gun butts reflecting dark light, riding comfortably and unsuspectingly toward the cañon's widening mouth.

Old Uriah Gorman watched them from his place of concealment while other crouched figures watched old Uriah. His head was well above the boulders, a strange white aura around it, star shine pointing out the unkemptness of his gray beard and white thatch of hair. It showed, too, the prominence of high cheek bones and the sunkenness of his eyes. He was a gaunt old man, better than six feet tall. His hands were dirt-ingrained, big, and liver-spotted. The one holding his carbine was scarred from fire; it was hairless and shiny. He moved that hand.

"Now!"

Guns came up amid the rocks and a series of traumatic explosions followed. The first cowboy went off his horse backward over the cantle. The second one had time to lift his head. Moonlight touched his face briefly; he was young and in the space of a heartbeat he was also dead. The third rider folded forward. His hat fell off and dark curly hair jerked wildly from impact. His horse went down with him. In six seconds three men and one horse had died.

Then silence returned.

Uriah got to his feet, peering northward toward the cañon's mouth. Two riderless horses trotted away on stiff legs. One snorted and yanked back, breaking the reins.

The other men stood up on both sides of old Uriah. One looked at the bodies and sank down upon a boulder. Another looked at his companions; they did not look back at him. Uriah went forward, big, gaunt, raw-boned, and poked at the corpses with his carbine. Somebody went back for their horses.

The spring was settled now and wild geese passed far above in perfect triangles, calling that winter was gone. Warm winds from Mexico met the frozen air of Canada and a good warmth resulted. It still froze at night but midday was pleasant. Game was returning, too, and the short grass made a green haze in sparkling distances. Within the stone fence was a low, rude house, part sod, part peeled logs. Beyond it was an ugly but functional barn. There were other buildings of log and mud—a farrowing pen, a woodshed, a bunkhouse.

Behind the bunkhouse and covering the big distance to the barn were pole corrals. Farther out, a long way off but looking closer because of the rare clear air, were Wyoming's Flint Hills, hard flanks squatting upon the flat flow of range, rising high in crumpled disarray and spiked with trees, mottled with brush, tilted and stony and barren.

Four men were driving gaunt cattle toward the corrals. Dun dust arose around them. They rode easy and slouched, warming sunlight upon their backs, then they halted and watched the cattle squeeze past the gate. The foremost man, grizzled in an old Cheyenne-tanned riding coat of nearly knee-length buckskin, worn and stained, looped his reins, stuffed a little pipe, jammed it between his teeth, and lit it. The smoke rose up and hung unmoving above his head.

When the last critter was through the gate the other riders converged on him. They were younger men, alike in sinewy lankness. One wore a pistol with an ivory handle. He also had silver conchos on his saddle. The others did not. Their guns were hard-rubber butted and their conchos were plain serrated leather. Before they were together the last man raised his head, hesitated a moment, then spoke.

"Someone's comin' . . . yonder there . . . to the south."

Each head swung and each face opened with quick interest.

7

The grizzled man puffed a moment, removed the pipe, and spat. "Where's the other two?" he asked of no one in particular.

The rider came up fast. Long before he was close, they could sense his urgency.

"Something went wrong," the older man said, a knife-edged sharpness coming into his voice.

Without a word they all rode toward the newcomer, passing the ranch house, the barn, bunkhouse, and a paralleling length of the stone fence on their right.

"It's Dade Simpson."

The grizzled man's pipe was cold in his mouth. He removed it, knocked it empty on the saddle horn, and pocketed it. When the rider slid down to a spewing halt before them, he said: "They got 'em, Paxton. Got 'em where the cañon comes out onto the prairie."

There was a heavy, long interval of silence, then Paxton Clement spoke past lips that scarcely moved: "Does your pa know, Dade?"

"He knows. He was with our riders when they found 'em." Dade looked at the four motionless men before him. "They were hid in the rocks. When Clint and Pete and Asa came out of the pass, they were waiting."

"It wasn't no fight . . . ?"

Dade shook his head. "All the shooting was done by the sheepmen. Our boys never got off a shot. Asa's horse and Pete's horse are loose somewhere on the range. Clint's horse is lying half atop him."

Paxton Clement looked as dark as thunder. His pale eyes were terrible to see but strangely his voice did not change from its knife-edged quietness. "All right, Dade," he said. "You tell your pa to get the others together and meet me at the cañon in a couple hours. . . . Bring spades. . . ."

Ezekiel Gorman was as tall as his father, old Uriah, but much heavier. At thirty years of age Ezekiel was no paradox. He was the best rifle shot among the sheepmen. He was taciturn, massive, gray-eyed, and shockle-headed like the old man. He was also as knife-lipped and uncompromising.

Zeke's brother—Robert Edward Lee Gorman, called Lee—was quiet like Zeke. He was only twenty-five to Zeke's thirty years. He was also different in other ways. Not only in the expression of his face, which was full-lipped and thoughtful, but in the way he shrank from violence.

Lee could outwork a horse at planting time. He could outwork two men at the hardest labor—at the shearing pens, during lambing season, at the dipping vats. But he was nearly useless in the face of this gathering storm for survival that had split the free-graze men of Wyoming—the cowmen and sheepmen. He stood with Zeke now, behind their father, listening to the talk of a swarthy, squat man wearing a stocking cap, fingers scrabbling along the seams of his trousers, eyes looking far out, and lips lying closed with bitter pressure, corners pulled down.

"I was hid like you said," the dark man was saying, liquid dark eyes fixed in fascination upon the gaunt old man standing like stone before him, like a prophet of old. "I saw 'em comin' and watched. It was Charley Simpson's crew from C Bar S. Was six of 'em. They came up and stopped and sat there for a minute just lookin' down . . ."

"And?" the old man prompted.

"They dragged 'em together and covered 'em with their slickers. Simpson sent four riders away. They rode in different directions . . . they rode hard, Uriah. . . ."

"Yes," the old man said, and bit it off. "To tell their friends. Then what?"

"Well, the others . . . the ones who stayed back . . . they went around behind the boulders and looked for sign. Finally Charley Simpson mounted up alone and commenced followin' your horse tracks. The other two, they were still with the bodies when I left to come up here and tell you."

"You did right," Uriah said, but his mind was turning away from the killing even then. "Now, you tell the others to stay close to their camps within sound of one another and wait. Now it's up to *them*. They killed Manuel Cardoza in his blankets and burned out the Shipman's Meadow camp and we give 'em back Pete Slocum, Clinton Hoag, and Asa Logan." The old man walked away.

Two years and two months before, in March of 1883, he had kneeled weeping at the mud bank of the Missouri where a worn-out drab woman lay wrapped in soiled canvas—Amethyst Gorman his wife, also from Virginia, dead at fifty-three. Dead of cholera it had been said, but, no, he knew better. She was dead of suffering, of hardship and persecution and extinguished hope.

"You boys spell off on keeping watch!" he called to Zeke and Lee. "They'll be a-coming."

He had been at Appomattox barefoot and with no crown in his straw hat, with a ration of parched corn in one pocket and eleven rifle cartridges in another pocket, a vanquished survivor of Major-General Stephan Ramseur's brigade of Jubal Early's Second Corps, Confederate Army.

He had arrived at Appomattox with his company the 1st of April, 1865—April Fool's day—when the Confederate States of America had eight days left to live. He had sat in silence with the others, back against a stone wall where worn-out rifles stood, watching the mass and the might of the blue North come up, endless ranks of men, miles of wagons laden with food, with medicine and clothing and good canvas tents—but mostly with shoes. The Confederacy had marched itself barefoot two years before. Shoes were as dear as victory and of late more obtainable.

Then home to Virginia, to Old Dominion Virginia not belly-crawling Yankee-loving West Virginia, but to loyal Confederate Virginia. Home to Amethyst and her soft fullness. Home to the soil and Reconstruction and Yankee occupation patrols riding through his thin crops with hard laughter. Home to desolation, to hopelessness. But he had been a stubborn man. He had gone down the rows seeding, stirring the soil with a broken hoe. His hands knew the way of it. All his life had been spent in the service of the earth, close to free-growing things and beasts. The best of his strength had been spent here. But then, with Amethyst suckling their youngest, and quick-growing Zeke burnished with the red dust of Virginia at the cabin stoop, Uriah's thoughts had gone beyond.

But Zeke was nigh as tall as the old man before they had finally cut the cord and begun their wandering. First to Alabama, then to Tennessee and finally to Missouri. Nearly fifteen years of it before they crossed the Missouri River heading for Wyoming Territory, and then, in the evening of his time, Uriah had buried Amethyst in alien soil, worn out from despair, dead not of cholera but of her soul's defeat.

He remembered telling Zeke at the first scent of trouble: "If you want to live you have to fight. Everywhere I've ever been it's like that.

Wyoming's no different from Virginia or Missouri. You've got to give as hard as you get, boy."

They had been clearing ground at this very sheep camp not six months before when a party of horsemen had ridden up, rough men in wide hats and wool shirts, heavily armed men with belt guns and carbines.

A grizzled wiry man had called sharply: "What the hell are you doing here?"

And Uriah's hot pride had answered up just as sharply: "We're setting up a sheep camp, stranger. We're newcomers who've joined up with the other sheepmen. That answer you?"

The grizzled man had sucked a moment on his pipe, and then he had said: "You'll find out soon enough whether it answers me or not, you god-damned sheepmen!"

The horsemen had spun away then, and from that moment on Uriah had known what lay ahead.

He had made his boys live with their rifles while he took to wearing again the scarred, long-barreled Dragoon revolver that had been his companion for more than twenty years.

Some of the sheepmen had sold out and gone. Those who remained the old man had tongue-lashed into an organization for mutual protection. It had been no simple accomplishment, and even now, because fear kept them close and their woolly bands had to range and re-range the same graze that was becoming increasingly poor, there was much talk against him even in the sheep camps.

Only two things kept the sheepmen from quitting altogether. One, it was not a rare thing to find a man dead in his sheep camp, shot through the heart at the lambing pens. Fear kept many from attempting to flee.

The other thing was two disastrous winters— 1884 had been an open winter, no snow pack to speak of and too dry and balmy. The following summer had seen drought and dying cattle. Then the winter of 1885 had come with unprecedented blizzards, snowdrifts ten feet high. Weakened cattle had died by the thousands. The cowmen had their backs to the wall. Many went down and the others were wavering. They had neither the money nor the time to fight Uriah's kind the way they ordinarily would have fought them—with hired killers and torch-bearing night riders. They were fighting for survival against the elements. One more unnatural winter would finish them.

It had been Paxton Clement of XIH who had said that salvation for the cowmen lay in keeping all the free range for themselves. He had told his neighbors if they could get their herds grease-fat by fall, they could weather another bad winter, but, if they could not, then they must face disaster.

Uriah knew about this. He knew there was a mote of truth in it. But he also knew that Paxton

Clement's hatred of sheepmen was a depthless thing; it would make him warp his reasoning to expedite a war. It had already driven him to send cowboys to raid sheep camps, to kill herders and club woollies to death by the score. It was, in Uriah's mind, the actual cause of the death of Asa Logan, Clinton Hoag, and Pete Slocum.

So, the old man stood apart, watching Zeke and Lee without really seeing them at work by the pens, letting gray thoughts claim him. The afternoon moved on; the sun went lower, throwing a bright yellow glitter over everything and as far as the eye could see was Wyoming—light-dappled mountains, purple-green and forested, an endless rise and tilt of flint hills and short-grass country.

He went to the sheep wagon and sank down there with an odd trembling in his legs, busy with the dark seeds of his mind, unmindful of the plaintive bleating along the side hills, unmindful of big Zeke's quick, sure motions at the pens or of gentle Lee's slumped posture and vacant long looks toward the horizon. Mindful only that the fighting had commenced.

He was so far lost in thought that Zeke called twice in his thundering voice before Uriah raised his head, then stood up.

"One man . . . comin' alone," Zeke said, standing massive in the puddling shadows, rifle crooked in one arm and his wealth of hair tumbling low. "Looks like a cowman."

Uriah went forward with a thrusting stride, head up and eyes fiercely open. This could not mean an attack, not one man riding up alone. It probably was the law.

The three of them stood like statues, waiting for the stranger to breast the hill and draw rein. When he did so, each of them saw the silver circlet on his shirt with the star inside it. It was a new kind of badge to them. Not until the rider was nodding did they make out the little letters: Deputy U.S. Marshal.

"Howdy, gents," the lawman said softly, noting each face, each expression, and each weapon. "My name's Garner. Burt Garner. I'm deputy U.S. marshal from Denver. . . . Mind if I get down?"

Uriah shook his head. "No, get down, stranger." That was all he said. No howdy, no welcome of any kind.

Garner stood near his horse's head, holding the reins. He was six inches shorter than any of the Gormans and he was between the ages of Zeke and the old man with a sprinkling of gray above the ears. He wore one black-butted, short-barreled gun around his belly and a carbine lay snug under the *rosadero* of his saddle. He was a level-eyed, impassive man, efficient and capable-looking. In the face of obvious hostility, a solid wall of it, he stood relaxed.

"You know about the killings," he said, making

a statement. "I'd like to hear what you know about them."

"Nothing," Uriah said. "Nothing at all."

After a moment of silence the marshal sucked his lips back, then blew outward. "I see. Well, there's talk sheepmen done it."

"If we'd all been in Saint Joe you'd have still heard that!" Uriah exclaimed.

Zeke broke in, his eyes full of challenge. "Is there also talk about dead sheep herders, clubbed sheep, and burned sheep camps, Marshal? No . . . you're god-damned right there isn't . . . not in the places where you hang out."

Garner looked away from Uriah. He studied Zeke with deliberation, then gazed at young Lee. His eyes lingered there the longest.

"The law doesn't take sides," he said finally to Zeke.

Uriah made a short, flat laugh. "No? Then why's the law dress like the cowmen? Why d'you wear cowmen's boots and pants and hat?"

"What you wear isn't important," Garner replied. "It's how you figure and act that counts."

He looked beyond to the wagon, then at the pens, and finally at the woolly shapes browsing through the hillside brush, and, although the smell was strong, he seemed not to notice it. He looked again at the three big men, standing motionlessly and charily before him.

"I was just passing through on my way back to

Denver from Laramie when I heard about the killings. Thought I'd sort of look around." He toed into the stirrup and sprang into the saddle. Now his impersonal stare was for Uriah exclusively. "They told me your name back in Union City, Mister Gorman. They told me a lot of other stuff too, but I didn't pay no attention to most of it. Still, when there's smoke there's usually some fire. That's how come I rode up here today to tell you not to start a range war."

"*Start* one . . . !" Zeke exploded.

Uriah's upflung arm stopped him. The old man nodded; he understood this kind of man. This quiet-talking level-eyed kind. He understood them perfectly. No quarter given or asked. No words wasted.

"We're going to fight only to protect what is ours, Marshal, you have my word on that. But . . . we'll wade to our hocks in blood to do that," he ended fiercely. "Law or no law."

"I think you already have," Marshal Garner stated, and wheeled away without a nod.

They watched him angle back down the sheep runs toward the flat country, each with different thoughts. Uriah put a hand out to touch his youngest son.

"Go saddle my horse, Lee. I think we'll have visitors in force at one of the camps tonight. I aim to pass the word to keep a close watch."

Lee went. Uriah watched him a moment, then

faced his eldest son. "Zeke, mind your brother while I'm gone. Stay out of the light and pay no mind to the call of sheep-killing coyotes tonight . . . the cowmen learned a lot from Indians."

"I'll watch," Zeke growled, still watching the diminishing figure far out over the range. "He sure didn't act like he was fixing to arrest anyone for Asa and Pete and Clint."

"He's got to have more than just three corpses, boy. He's got to have witnesses, at least."

"Those," Zeke said with emphasis, "he'll never get if I'm along."

Uriah bobbed his head. "Just you remember that, Son. A dead man never hung anybody."

Chapter Two

Logan, Hoag, and Slocum were buried. The law had come into the hills. Not just Deputy U.S. Marshal Burt Garner from Denver, but Town Marshal Will Harper from Bethel—who owned two large bands of sheep and hired Basques to herd them—and another town marshal, Bob Ander from Union City, the cowmen's stronghold. Ander made it plain what he thought, but attempted no arrests. Neither had fat Will Harper, but then he wouldn't have anyway.

Uriah Gorman had met with the other sheepmen, and had found most of them sunk in remorse, and fearful. It made him sick, he said.

19

The cowards could kill from ambush but that was the end of their courage.

"Guts," he told Zeke and Lee. "It's a man's guts that make the difference between a sniper and a bushwhacker. One's got 'em, t'other hasn't."

He flung his saddle down and flagged the horse away from camp with a big hand. Overhead, a lop-sided, yellow moon filled the world with ugly light. It was warm and still. From the pens came restless bleats but for the most part there was a hush.

"Go on to bed," Uriah said to his boys. "I'll set out here for a spell, then I'll be along."

But hours passed before he stirred. He sat there hunched in the night's stillness, hair awry as it always was, great beard splayed out stiff from the unconscious combing of bent fingers, stained trousers and shirt in near tatters, long feet encased in old cracking boots, strong-smelling and raw-boned, bent over by the dying fire like an aged, defeated dirt farmer—until you saw his face, the gray-green eyes with something wild-like showing, and something faintly brooding, the iron thrust of jaw, and the mouth sucked down in bitterness. There was something more to him, then, than his appearance of poverty. There was a vitality, an urgency you could not describe or grasp, but you felt it. Sitting there now, with a faint, acrid scent of black-oak embers in his nostrils, he brooded alone.

Something would be done. Something had to be done. The bands were diminishing, the graze was low, and the cowmen hedged them around. And quickly, because the cowmen would grow stronger as they, the sheepmen, grew weaker.

Today two more had given up—Schwartz and Koeppfler. Dutch immigrants, true, but sheepmen nonetheless and each one who quit burdened those who remained with heavier loads. Something had to be done.

There could be no appeal to justice. The simple fact was that Wyoming had no justice, not in the mountains or out upon the prairies. It didn't have but one white man to the mile, and two-thirds of those were cowmen or their hirelings. (In six years, when Wyoming would become a state, it would still have only two people per square mile.)

Fight! Uriah thought. *Fight them in the mountains and out upon the prairies. From the Flint Hills to their door stoops. Fight them till hell freezes over and for ten days on the ice!*

There was nothing else to do. Unless they fought now they'd be broken later. The cowmen surrounded them, kept their sheep from the plains, raided their camps, and killed their herders when they tried to break clear of the mountains. They poisoned water holes and stampeded their woollies over cliffs, resisted every effort the sheepmen made to survive.

Uriah stirred, rubbed circulation into one leg.

It wasn't only the cowmen who could not afford another bad winter; sheep froze to death, also. But sheep could survive where cattle couldn't—*if* they had access to brush browse. Cattle would stand and bawl and lie down like dumb brutes in the midst of a thicket and die. Not sheep. They'd bleat protest, but, before they'd give up, they'd eat the thicket to survive.

Fight! Uriah thought with a wild fullness running through him. *One man could overturn the universe if he fought for right . . . for survival. If justice was framed into unjust laws, then we must fight the law. If the government, in the form of steady-eyed Burt Garner, upheld injustice, then we must resist the government, too. There is a higher law.*

The wildness mounted in the old man's heart. His strange eyes burned with unshed tears. Fight! *They* would come again, this time in retaliation, and this time sheepmen would die. That was right. He would not lift a hand to stop it because it would make the sheepmen band together. They would come to him and he would lead them.

When the cowmen came this time there *would* be war. From this time on.

He left the dead fire, went to his blankets, and sank down, weary of body but fierce in mind. He did not sleep. Overhead a million stars flickered, congealed tears shed by a ravished universe. Appomattox . . . Reconstruction . . . Alabama . . .

Tennessee. Amethyst and the Missouri River bottoms . . . Wyoming . . . A man could live with defeat but he never ceased to struggle against it so long as breath remained. Happiness? Hope? Who was he to hope, to be happy, Uriah Gorman of Virginia. Remember that: Uriah Gorman of Virginia, battler against oppression, Yankee or cowman oppression.

Morning came. The weather was balmy. Columbine and lupine showed against the rich soil. Zeke and Lee had let the sheep out. They were drinking their second cup of coffee when their father returned from the creek, face shiny-cream and youthful-looking, only the eyes unchanged, being slightly bloodshot and a little wilder-looking than they had been the day before.

He ate in silence as was his custom. Zeke and Lee waited. He was finishing when the wagon hove into view down below the camp.

"Looks like Amaya's outfit," Zeke said.

They paid no more attention to the wagon. Pedro Amaya was a Mexican sheepman from Arizona. He was a diffident person, the color of saddle leather, and, when he spoke, he smiled apologetically. They called him Pete and he was a good sheepman. He had been at the rocks with the others when Slocum, Hoag, and Logan had died.

Lee cleaned up the breakfast mess. He was stowing tin plates and cups in the side box of the camp wagon when Pete Amaya's team breasted the last lift of the trail and grunted on to the plateau. Lee went back where Zeke and Uriah stood watching the wagon grind toward them. Uriah was motionless. When he spoke it was in a low tone.

"He isn't smiling."

Amaya drew up, looped his lines, and got down heavily. He faced the three Gormans only a moment, then he nodded without speaking and walked back along the wagon. Uriah saw him lift a canvas and stare downward. He went forward, followed by his sons.

"It is Evans and Buell," Amaya said quietly.

Uriah looked at the frozen faces and the blood-stained clothing. Beside him Zeke sucked back a sharp breath. Lee turned away.

Amaya dropped the canvas. "Their bands did not come to water this morning. I went over to see was ever'thing all right. . . ." A shrug.

"Didn't you hear any shooting in the night?" Uriah demanded.

"I hear nothing. Nothing at all."

Amaya removed his hat, swiped a grimy sleeve across his forehead, and replaced the hat. He was looking out over the plain below. "It could have been me."

"Who else knows?"

"No one. Your camp was closest. I come here with them."

"Zeke," Uriah barked, "ride to the other camps. Tell 'em we got a burying to attend to. Go on!"

They left the wagon in the sun and went down by the pens to wait. Hours passed; gloom was heavy over the camp. Pete Amaya sat, motionless and silent, his eyes fixed on the far curve of earth. When the others began riding in, nothing changed much. The men stood about, strained and restless, sharing the common deep fear in vague talk.

Like their own sheep, Uriah thought, *milling around, peeking at the corpses, leaderless.* He got up, sent Lee for faggots, and told him to make fresh coffee. Zeke was there, and he helped.

"Over here!" old Gorman called, and waited for them to approach the cooking fire's stone ring. Eleven of them, counting Pedro Amaya who still hadn't moved. *Eleven sheepmen more like sheep than men. Well, from this time on they will be men,* Uriah said to himself.

"You saw!" he thundered at them. "They come in the night like coyotes . . . like cowards. They killed Lester Evans and Carter Buell. They've killed others. They'll kill us all in time. . . ."

Beside and below him Lee made the fire, keeping his head down. Zeke stood back with the black coffee pot, harkening to his father's wrath, thrilled to the heart by it. Of them all he was most under Uriah's spell. He would do whatever Uriah told him, anything at all at any time.

"We're human beings. . . . We've got a right to

live. . . . Do we have to wear crowns of thorns because we're sheepmen . . . ?"

He played them, touched their rawest nerves, bolstered their courage, and drained away the fear and timidity.

"We can kill, too. . . . We've got to kill. It's kill or be killed. We can't run . . . we can't hide . . . we can't leave with only the rags on our backs. From now on we've got to give as good as we get. We've got to give *better* than we get . . . !"

Lee straightened up when the fire was going. He moved back to let Zeke move forward and place the pot over the stones. His face was white. Words formed in his head. *Don't do it, Father. Don't kill them in cold blood. It'll make you as low as they are. Find another way. You're talking these men into dying. Father, don't do it!*

A slight man with a scraggly fawn-colored moustache and intense black eyes interrupted Uriah. "We got to fight, yes . . . but how?"

"The same way they do!" Uriah roared. "With the night as our ally. With guns and torches!"

A bottomless hush came. Men stirred. They looked away from the elder Gorman. They looked at one another. They thought a hundred thoughts but his hold was on them. Their blood was running full. They muttered: "Yes . . . the same way *they* do. Yes."

They cheered Uriah. They struck one another across the shoulders. They felt good. Like men.

Like *real* men. Even Pedro Amaya's despair was gone; his teeth flashed white and a cruel light shone from his eyes. "¡*Seguro!*" he cried into the shouts. "We fight . . . *los vengadores, sí, sí.*" The conflicting heritages of Castile and Anahuac moved in Amaya; his diffidence vanished; he drew a pistol and flourished it. "We follow Uriah . . . we fight back!"

"Get your horses!" Uriah called over the noise. "Your horses and your guns."

Their voices diminished. They looked toward him, flush-faced and eager.

"XIH brought us to this and, by God, XIH will harvest what it's sown. Get your horses . . . let's go!"

They moved swiftly away. No one had touched Zeke's coffee. Uriah started toward the wagon where his rifle was. He passed Lee, standing alone, white and tortured. He stopped to throw his youngest a quick look.

"Take Amaya's wagon to Bethel. . . . No, no. Take it to Union City. Take it where the cowmen's womenfolk can see what's been done. Let Bob Ander see, too. Let everyone see what happens to people who want only to live . . . to . . ."

He didn't finish. The others were mounted and calling for him. He pushed on by, went into the wagon, grabbed up the rifle, rummaged for shells, then returned into the sunlight. There was a spring in his step; the awry hair and gray beard jerked with each movement of his body. He was a young man again. He was hastening toward Bull Run, toward victory.

They clattered down off the plateau trailed by a pall of thick dust. Sunlight winked off their armament. They rode straight in the saddle with the roar of blood in their ears. As the sounds of their passing atrophied, plaintive bleating filled the hush. Lee heard.

He watched until even the dust was gone, then he went to the stone ring and filled a cup with coffee. His father was wrong; he'd seen him wrong before and on those occasions he'd tried to meet the old man's green-burning gaze. But he never could. The other's will was stronger. Even when he struggled the hardest, he knew he was lost. At times his bitterness and anguish were almost hatred for his father.

He didn't want to wander the earth, to run from memories. He wanted to put down roots, to live and let live. To grow things from the soil. He didn't want a bullet or a hemp rope. He wanted to plant corn and watch it tassel out, to coax life into newborn lambs, to build a cabin with his hands. . . .

He went to the wagon, climbed up, untwisted the lines, and flicked them without a backward glance at the rumpled canvas. He drove down off the plateau and cut northwest like he'd been told to do—toward the cowmen's town of Union City.

All morning the wagon creaked along over the plains. It was hot, away from the mountains. He was without cover and a burning sun was on him. He knew the bodies that jounced behind his back were swelling. The team raised dust in dun clouds, choking dust. He got thirsty and detoured toward Cottonwood Creek.

There was a sullen glow over the prairie, a sallowness hurting to the eye, a painful glare that quivered like jelly when he strained to see ahead where the creek showed glassy, dark, and sullen. There grew a fringe of slim willows along the spongy bank, and, as he let the team plod close and drink, he smelled oak-wood smoke. It would be coming from the Foster place over the near rise of land, easterly.

He didn't alight right away. The team made gulping sounds, sucking water around their bits. It was a good sound on a hot day. It was good, also, to be in among the green willows.

He got down finally, went ahead and kneeled to drink. It was the sound of a shod horse crossing rock that wrenched him upright, fear souring his stomach. The rider was approaching leisurely. He pushed willows aside to see better—and his legs went loose with relief. It was Ann Foster, youngest daughter of Lew and Molly Foster, the squatters who had a place beyond the creek and over the land swell. She was coming toward the creek bottom where coolness lay, thick enough to bend. He moved through the shade toward her, saw her dismount to water her horse, and drew up straighter. He could not help but notice the fullness of her figure before he spoke.

"Hello, Ann."

She spun, and when she replied, saying his name, it squirted out of her mouth sharp-sounding. "Lee!" There was a sheen of sweat on her forehead, her upper lip, and the darkness of her gaze was wide and all-seeing. She seemed scarcely to breathe. The fullness of her blouse, jutting and heavy, was stilled. "You put a scare into me."

"I expect I did," he said, listening to her horse sucking water. "You like to give me a start, too." He moved closer. "You looking for your paw's cattle?"

"Not the cattle, our sheep. I was up at the saltlick and got thirsty. It's hot today."

"Cooler in here all right," he agreed, feeling the drying sweat under his shirt cooling his flesh.

"What're you doing down here?"

"Got thirsty. I'm on my way to Union City."

She blinked thick lashes at him. "Union City . . . ?"

He glanced at the drinking horse, moved up to the very edge of the creek where the soil was spongy, and stood looking across, where cloud shadows spotted the endlessness of heat-dancing land.

"Lee? You in trouble, or something?"

He faced around to look at her in an unblinking way. "Trouble? Seems like that's about all there is, here."

She turned away from the slow-changing look in his eyes. "Not right here," she murmured. "It's peaceful along the creek. Sometimes I come here just to sit and daydream."

"Ann . . . you're sure pretty standing there like that."

She tugged at the horse's reins. "Shame on you, Lee . . . talking like that."

"No, it's nothing to be ashamed of. You really are pretty, there."

"You hadn't ought to say that, though."

"I guess I hadn't," he said, and reached for the horse's reins. She relinquished them. He tied the beast and touched her arm. "Walk with me along the creek."

She looked up quickly. There was nothing in Lee Gorman's face to cause fear or anger. She'd known him almost a year and had never seen anything wrong in his face. Uriah was different and so was Zeke—but Lee was sound.

They walked, twisting through the rank growth of willows following the creek and the lean shade along its bank, and beneath the straining cloth of her blouse the girl's heart beat solidly. A girl knew things like an animal knew them, by instinct. Ann Foster was like that. She breathed deeply of the

31

fragrant warm spring air full of flower scent, and walked beside him, all quiet and wary and willing. All still inside and tremulous.

They stopped in a tiny clearing where clumps of creek grass grew like toadstools, making shaggy hummocks. He sank down, her beside him, and looked into the dark-lashed eyes. "I wish I could tell you how it is with me, Ann," he said. "I wish I could tell someone."

The black watchfulness of her stare, the utter stillness of her face troubled him. He started to get to his feet.

"Lee?"

"Yes."

"Tell me. I'll listen."

"I guess not, Ann. I guess it's foolish the way I feel. The old man thinks it is . . . so does Zeke."

"Then I'll tell *you* something," she said with sudden force. "Of the three Gormans you're the least likely to be foolish."

He let himself fully down again and blinked at her, tried not to notice the way she sat on one of the hummocks with her skirt drawn tightly around the curve of hip.

"You're different, Lee. You *think* . . . your paw and big Zeke don't."

"Yes, they do," he answered loyally. "We think different is all. Paw's a fighter . . . been fighting all his life. Zeke . . . he fights, too."

"Fights what?"

"Oh, things inside him. Things he feels. I know. I know Zeke pretty well." He watched her profile. It was stoically unchanged and unchanging. "You don't understand me, do you?"

"I understand," she said in a low and bitter way. "Lots of folks understand, Lee. Zeke's a man fighter. Just a man fighter."

"I guess I'm the one that doesn't understand, Ann."

"Don't you? Your paw . . . he's got Zeke wrapped around his finger. He won't fight it and he can't break it. That's what I mean. Folks notice those things, Lee. They talk about them. Not just the cowmen but the squatters, too. They see how things are." She turned her head so she could see his damp face in the drawn-out light of willow shadows. "Maybe you don't know these things. I reckon you don't. You don't look like you do."

"I know them," he said heavily, and let it die there.

She sat there gazing at him a moment before she spoke again. "What were you going to tell me, Lee?"

"Nothing."

There was something hard and unpleasant in the glade with them now. The mellowness was gone. He looked straight ahead.

She bent forward, touched his bare neck with her fingers. "I want to hear it. I want you to tell me, Lee."

At her touch fresh sweat burst out between his shoulder blades. "I wish I could," he said hoarsely. "I'd like to tell somebody sometime . . . just to get it out of me."

The fingers worked his damp flesh, kneading it like bread dough until he had to move out of her reach and her hand fell back to her side. Then words came out of him with a big burst of breath.

"I want to leave, Ann. That's all. . . ." He looked at her face. There was no change in it. She remained impassive, dark eyes still and bottomless. The wide swell of her mouth closed without pressure, full and shiny.

"Go on," she said, low.

"Get some land somewhere and grow things."

"Yes."

"Make an orchard, build a house, get some sheep and cows and pigs, and grow things. Be neighborly with folks. I don't want to be fighting all the time . . . be hated and full of hate."

"Your paw'd shoot you if he heard this," she said.

"Well, that's how it is, anyway. I don't like to go to Bethel or Union City. I know what folks think . . . especially the ranchers. Ann, I don't hate them."

"A stone house near a creek, Lee?"

He nodded, blood running under his cheeks. "About like that."

"With a root cellar and a place to put down salt

meat and apples, and eggs in a crock . . . and a woman?"

His color flooded beet red.

"To lie with . . . ?"

He jumped up sweating. "Ann, you shouldn't talk like that!"

She jumped up just as swiftly, her back very straight, cheeks white, and eyes blazing with candor. "You got rams with your ewes . . . we got bulls with our cows. How'll you have young ones without a woman, Lee? They go with the house and the creek and the root cellar and all. You know that."

"But you shouldn't talk about it, though."

"Why not, it's natural, isn't it?"

He didn't answer; he just looked at her and swallowed hard.

"Lee?"

"Yes, Ann."

"When're you going to do it . . . go away?"

"I don't know. It's what I want to do. I haven't any plans though. Not yet."

She swung away, then back again, and he was surprised at the strange, urgent expression she wore now. There was something secretive in her face—something cunning—like she was smoothing out an idea, perfecting it as she stared at him.

"Do you know what Zeke and Emily Potter did the night of the Fourth of July dance, Lee?"

He didn't know, so he said nothing.

"I reckon that wasn't wrong, was it?"

"You're talking strange," he husked. "I never heard you talk like this before."

"No, you haven't. But you only ride over when your paw sends you after rock salt." She looked past him at the sluggish moving water. "People got to grow up sometime, don't they? Learn to see things different. Not good or bad but like they really are."

"Well," he stammered in the face of her strangeness, her sudden vitality. "Anyway, I feel better for telling you how it is with me, Ann. . . ." He was trying to get things back the way they had been but the black fire in her stare blinded him. His words trailed off into nothing.

She was very close to him, so close the rise and fall of her blouse swayed against his shirt front. There was a challenge in her face as clear as day, as inviting as a cool spring.

"I want to get away, too, Lee. Far away . . . even out of Wyoming." She spoke almost fiercely.

"You . . . do?"

"Clean away. And have things of my own. A stone house by a creek. I've pictured it in my mind for a long time. With critters around and young ones."

She took his hand and pressed it in the valley of her breasts and leaned up against him like that, with the tall thin shadows mottling them and the curse of unhappiness a deep physical pain in them both.

Lee made no move to retreat; he was rooted. A spiral of warmth uncoiled in him, thrust upward and upward and he finally forgot what, exactly, he was doing in the glade and thought only of the agonizing want that was there in the silence with them, beside the muddling creek. He touched her hair with his free hand. Let it wind through the blackness, fingers like brown worms groping without sight. Then he dropped the hand lower, to her neck, to her shoulder, and let it hang there, sweat-slippery and trembling.

She was as still as stone but the hard thrust when she breathed burst against him and he knew there was more than just his own fever between them. He kept his hand upon her shoulder, afraid, almost sick with fear, with knees that trembled and with sweat that ran and nearly blinded him.

She bit her lip and it hurt. Not enough to make her cry but she cried anyway, softly. Racking deep but softly, and, when he moved back a little, she sank down limply on the grass hummock and covered her face with her hands and just cried.

"Ann . . . ?"

He was miserable. Everything else was forgotten—the ripening bodies under the tarp in the wagon, the sheepmen riding to XIH with Uriah, the perils of Union City. He was long-faced, as white as a sheet with his mouth hanging slack, heavy lids half covering his eyes.

"Lee . . . are you ashamed?"

"Yes."

"I'm not!"

She wiped her face. It felt hot. She pressed both palms against her cheeks and looked up at him. Her eyes were twice as black as he'd ever seen them. There was a hot luster to them from shed tears.

"You cried . . ."

"I don't know why, Lee. Maybe because when you want something a lot and it comes close you can't stand it."

"Want what?"

"That stone house by the creek and the man who'll make it for me."

He stared down at her.

"That's why I cried. Lee? Don't stare at me. Lee? Will you kiss me? I want you to kiss me."

When he didn't move, she reached up, caught his hands, and pulled him down upon the grass, got close to him, put both hands on his head, and kissed him on the mouth, on the lips, pulled back six inches, and looked at him and smiled, then kissed him again.

He couldn't remember ever having seen Ann Foster smile before although he had seen her smile because he'd known her since they'd come to the flint hills country. He just hadn't noticed, particularly, before.

Finally she drew off a little and said: "I've got some jerky in my saddlebags. Shall I get it?"

"I couldn't eat it," he said honestly.

Her head bent forward again. She murmured— "This is food."—and kissed him again, pressing wide lips over his mouth, holding him in a velvet grip so that he couldn't have torn free if his life had depended upon it. Then she lay her head against him and the furry quiver of her breath touched his cheek, and he felt with his hands, locking them around her.

"I know how a bird feels when you hold it in your hand," she said softly. "Now I know exactly how it feels." She took one of his hands free. "Do you feel my heart?"

"Yes."

She put her head upon his chest. "And yours . . ."

"I don't feel right, Ann."

"Scared?"

"More'n just scared. Like this is wrong."

She made a hard short shake of her head and the lash of her hair made his skin prickle. "No it isn't, Lee. I thought so, too, for a while, but now I know it's not wrong. We've got a right to fight for what we want. That's not wrong."

"Well, no," he said. "*That* isn't . . . but *this* might be."

"No, not even this. Your paw, my paw, Zeke, my sister, the folks in Union City and Bethel . . . they don't exist right now, Lee. There's no one in the world this minute but you and me, and what we do with each other is right. That's what I knew when

I kissed you. What you and I do together is right." She raised up and plucked at his shirt where it lay soggily over his chest. "You're sweating like a stud horse."

"I have reason."

She stiffened the length of her, drew back, got to her feet, and reached forward to tug him up off the ground. "Come along. Down here a ways."

The creek slapped torpidly against some gray sand. Sunshine exploded off shiny pebbles and the ground underfoot was resilient.

"Lie down there. No, take your shirt off first."

"What for?"

But he removed it and the breadth of his chest was immense, swelling upward and outward from lean flanks corded and thick from labor, but paler than his wrists and face where the sun had left its shades.

"Now lie down there . . . on your stomach."

She scooped up water in her hands and washed his back with slow, circling motions. Bent over him and leaned with her upper body swaying until his head, lying over his arms, grew limp and began to sway, too.

It was wonderful. It was relaxing and blissful. He let his body run loose against the earth its full length. Neither of them spoke for a long time. Until the shadows had moved a little south and west. Then she kissed him between the shoulder blades, up along the neck, and he rolled over to reach for her with all the fright gone. Touched her with the tremors stilled, the doubts and quaking forgotten, and she smiled tenderly at him.

"Lee . . . didn't you ever guess?"

He heard through a redness and didn't care what she said, what anyone said, even his paw. Nothing existed for him but the bigness of her eyes, growing bigger until she closed them.

Chapter Three

He left her when the marching shadows were lengthening easterly, drove the full distance to Union City and left the corpses of Lester Evans and Carter Buell lying in the dust beside the plank walk and drove the long way back, arriving at the foot of the plateau after midnight with a stained circlet of silver riding high overhead.

From far out he had seen the shifting tongue of orange flame, larger than a cooking fire, at their camp. It meant, of course, that there were others on the plateau as well as his father and brother.

It was hard to force his mind back to Uriah and Uriah's way. For the first time since he could remember Uriah and Zeke were not uppermost in his thoughts.

Even while he had been arranging the corpses in the dust of Union City's roadway, saying nothing nor looking up at the ring of white, shocked faces, he had not thought of his peril there.

The team braced to the collar. Chain tugs clanked and the wagon started upward. Above, someone called sharply. Lee heard but did not heed. When he topped out and drew up, there was a small mob of armed men standing ready and looking at him. Uriah pushed through, trailing his rifle. Beyond, the fire burned wickedly, darkly, throwing out shadows that jerked and panted.

"You all right, boy?"

He looped the lines. "I'm all right."

Pedro Amaya looked in the bed of the wagon under the canvas. "They're gone," he said flatly.

"Didn't no one offer to stop you?" someone asked on a rising note.

Lee got down. "No. I drove into town, put them out in the roadway before the marshal's office, and drove out again. I don't recollect anyone saying anything."

Zeke was moving up slowly, puzzled-looking and straining to see his brother's face. When Uriah would have spoken, Zeke brushed past him, leading Lee toward the big fire. Behind them Pedro Amaya was caring for his horses and the others were murmuring together.

There was rye whiskey and black coffee and fried mutton. Lee ate steadily. Zeke drank from a tin cup. His face was freshly washed but the strain still showed.

"What's the matter with you?" the elder brother asked over the rim of the cup.

Lee drank deeply and his head cleared. "Tired," he said. "Feel like I been drawed through a knothole. . . . What happened at XIH?"

Zeke put his cup down carefully and looked into it. "Nothing. Not a blamed thing. We rode out there and the place was as deserted as an empty gut. Pete picked up the sign and we tracked 'em to the glass rock this side of Simpson's C Bar S. There Pete lost the sign, but that made no difference. They were all at the Simpson place. From a hill we could see the rigs in the yard. Looked like every cowman in the country was there." Zeke raised his big head. Firelight flickered redly and sooty shadows lay in the hollows under his eyes. "You know what that powwow means, don't you?"

"War," Lee said succinctly.

"Yeah." Zeke picked up the cup, drained it, and tossed it aside. "That's what we been setting around here for. That, and wondering what had happened to you. Paw's been egging them to saddle up with him and ride to Union City to find you. He was sure they'd gotten you."

"No," Lee replied thickly, slowly. "I took my time. It was hot. . . ."

Zeke, watching his face, saw something there, something he could not define. He had seen it back by the wagon, too, but his big body ached and his soul had been drained dry by the day's excitement. He was too weary to be curious.

"What's he going to do now?" Lee asked idly, sinking lower against the earth with a delicious sense of languor stealing over him, feeling detached from Zeke and Uriah and the others.

"We're going back tonight and be in position by sunup."

"At XIH?"

Zeke nodded, firelight making his face sweat shiny. In a thick voice he added: "They want a fight, don't they?"

Dark ghostly shadows approached the fire. Pete Amaya lifted the jug of rye whiskey and drank, cursed softly in Spanish, and handed the jug around. A few laced their coffee with the stuff but not all. They all looked as gray-faced as big Zeke, with shifting, reddened eyes and wet mouths. Uriah's beard, russet in the firelight, was more unkempt than usual; his uncombed white thatch stood stiffly with sweat and dust. Where he squatted, rifle against his legs, lay a square-hewn trembling shadow.

"We figured they might've got you," he said to his youngest.

"It was hot. I drove slow."

"See any riders?"

"Not a one, Paw."

"You eaten?"

"Yes."

"Then fetch your musket from the wagon, saddle your horse, and let's go."

"Paw . . ."

Uriah was on his feet, moving away from the fire with the others, his voice rumbling at them. Zeke, across the fire, looked steadily at his brother, then he arose, also, and moved off after the others. Lee lay there, twisted from the waist, watching them. Then he got up and went toward the wagon.

Uriah led them down off the plateau and out along the mottled roadway. There was very little talk until they cut through a wild, timbered region westerly, leaving the wagon ruts behind. Then voices rose, some uneasy, some needlessly loud and hollow sounding. They came to another roadway, raw-cut and fresh with newness. It was a bad narrow brace of ruts with holes a foot deep in places, and jutting big rocks on either side, but it was well shielded by night and tall trees. It was the XIH's own lane. Uriah rode ahead, rifle balanced against his saddle swells, bony shoulders sharply pointed in the pale gloom, head up and moving constantly from side to side. After a long spell he drew up. The others halted behind him; their voices dwindled. Silence came. The deep, abiding silence of late night. Then Uriah left the road, pushed as far as an erosion slash, and swung down.

"We'll wait here for sunup," he said, and off-saddled.

There was a creeping iciness in the gully. In an

hour, when the whiskey wore off, they would all be shivering from the cold. Lee wrapped a sweat-stiff saddle blanket around his shoulders and sat, cross-legged, his mind miles away under the vivid hot sun of the creek bottom.

He scarcely heard Uriah call Pete and Zeke to him. There were other voices around him, muttering, but the old man's low burning tone was unmistakable in the darkness.

Lee must have slept because the pain in his crossed legs was fearful when he straightened up to look around.

Day had come with a boding sky and ashen mists that hurried before a low and fitful wind. Stiff bodies came up off the ground. Gray faces made evil by beard stubble and pouched eyes, swung left and right. Lee counted them. Including himself there were fourteen sheepmen in the gully.

They ate jerky and washed the salt away at a seepage spring. Uriah sent Pete Amaya creeping through the trees to spy on the Clement Ranch, which lay a long half mile beyond the farthest spit of timber. He and a sheepman named Fawcett sat together in desultory conversation. Between words Fawcett sucked on a pipe with deliberate, bubbling sounds. There were flecks of yellow spittle at the outer corners of Fawcett's lips. He seemed to be brooding and his impassivity came of natural lack of feeling, but Uriah, just as motionless, was leashed stillness. His hands holding the rifle were as still as stone, his sunken green eyes showed fire points of resolution. But unless you saw his eyes, you would have thought him a dejected fool-hoe man lashed to rawhide toughness by the same adversity that had broken his spirit. Only his eyes showed that this was not so and never would be so.

The others sat huddled against the scudding cold of the keening wind with rye whiskey dead in them, gray-faced, slack-mouthed, and dumb. *Like sheep,* Lee thought. *Exactly like sheep, waiting with immeasurable humility to be led or driven. Doing Uriah's bidding, never questioning his way, now that he had brought them down to this, just waiting patiently to be driven over a cliff or clubbed down or strung up and shot, but in the end totally mesmerized and completely under the old man's dominance.*

He knew Joseph Fawcett. He also knew George Dobkins and Kant U'Ren, the surly dark half-blood herder from Idaho who went insane when drunk, but who sat there now like a brown, carved harbinger of evil, brawny shoulders hunched forward, staring at the ground like a dumb brute. And farther back wiry Gaspar Pompa, the Basque, a friendly little man as active as a monkey and as simple in the head.

He knew them all, had known them for a year or better. Knew them inside and out. They were as transparent to him as the bright and gleaming water of life itself. When Pete returned and Uriah got up with his rifle, they would also get up with their rifles. Sheep-like, they would follow him through the trees to the attack.

"Boy, don't look like that."

He jerked around. Big Zeke dropped down beside him upon the frosted earth and let off a big breath. His breath smelled foul. Zeke had his rifle, held carelessly, and he didn't look at Lee when he spoke.

"It's got to be, that's all. Them or us. You know that." The big head turned and tilted. Eyes like Uriah's eyes looked from beneath thick brows. But they were simply calm, green-flecked eyes. They lacked the strangeness, the increasing wildness of Uriah's look.

"I guess so."

Zeke wiggled, reached under, and brushed aside a stone, then settled back again. He spat.

"Zeke?"

"Huh?"

"You . . . uh . . . seen Emily Potter lately?"

Zeke looked around. "No," he said. "Why do you ask that?"

"Not since the Fourth of July dance?"

Zeke straightened up a little, propped his body half up with his elbows. His gaze was unblinking. After an interval of silence he said: "You know, don't you?"

"Yes."

48

Zeke's eyes dropped. Color ran under his cheeks and his voice became gruff. "Well, just so long as the old man don't know. . . ."

"He won't."

"You seen her, Lee?"

"No. Not lately. Zeke, I want to know something. Did it mean anything to you?"

"Not with her, no. She's like her sister. She'd climb into the back seat of anyone's wagon. So would her sister. Don't either of 'em have any notion of fidelity. They're farm-girl chippies, Lee, that's all. I plumb pity the man who marries either of 'em. They'll be lying and cheating all their lives. You take the way they dress . . . ribbons and face rouge and all . . . it don't fool men very long."

Lee's palms grew slippery; anguish filled him. "I guess a girl who'd do that before she's married is no good, huh?"

"That's what folks say," said Zeke. "I don't rightly know. This I do know . . . a girl who sneaks out after she's married is lower'n the meanest man alive. When a woman can't be true to her man, she's the rottenest thing on this earth." Zeke looked up suddenly to study his brother's face, and the words on his lips died. He drew upright on the ground, crossing his legs. "Boy, who were you with today?" he sharply demanded.

"Not me, Zeke. I went . . ."

"You're lying, Lee. It's written all over your face."

Lee's voice sank to a corn-husk whisper. "It was different than the way you're talking, though."

"How different? Married woman or single?"

"Single."

"Do I know her?"

"Yes."

Zeke looked around them and lowered his voice. "Who?"

"Ann Foster."

Zeke looked surprised. "Ann?"

"Yesterday, Zeke, on the way to town. I met her along the creek below their place."

The older man's shoulders slumped. He rocked forth and back a moment before he spoke again. "I didn't know *she* was like that."

"She isn't. This was different."

Zeke continued to rock. After a while he said: "That's why you were so late."

"Yes."

"Paw'll skin you alive if he finds out."

"He won't."

"No? What if she comes up calvy? Her paw'll know, then the old man'll know . . . then everyone'll know."

"I hope she does, Zeke," the younger man said in a hard, fierce whisper.

Zeke bent a long stare on his brother. "You got it bad, haven't you?" He picked up his rifle and gazed at it unseeingly. "Hubs of hell," he muttered under his breath, then louder: "How long you been seeing her?"

"Well, never before like this." Lee picked up a crumbly rock and broke it between his fingers. "I'd never hardly talked to her before. At dances, sure, and when we go for rock salt, but that's about all." He let the stone fall away. "Yesterday . . ."

"Yeah?"

"I can't explain it, Zeke. I got her inside me . . . in my head. I just can't think about anything else." He made a tight motion with one hand. "Even this . . . what we're waiting to do . . . don't seem real to me."

Zeke stopped rocking. His bushy brows were drawn down hard in a thunderous look. He said no more until a slight stir among the other waiting men snagged his attention. Then he shook his head like a bull at fly time and twisted to look behind him. Pete Amaya was cat-footing it through the misty raw light of dawn. Uriah was getting up stiffly. Zeke gathered up his gun and rolled to his feet. "Come on," he said gruffly, without looking at Lee. "It's time to go."

Uriah led them after one flaming look and one spoken admonition: "Go quiet, men . . . no talking and keep your guns up and ready."

He stalked ahead northward through the trees. Behind him came the ghostly company, like murk in the gray mist of early morn. At a churning creek with a rind of frost along its banks Uriah waited.

Then he plunged in unmindful of the freezing shock and waded across. Pete Amaya, stalking along beside the Basque, smiled broadly when Pompa gasped and swore in a shrill whisper. The water was like ice.

The timber began to thin out. They came to the dead-end of a stone fence. Beyond was a big clearing—a grain field not yet sown and with last summer's stubble standing stiffly dead and upright in it. They followed Uriah across this clearing trying to be quiet but hearing doubly loud the swish of stubble against their legs.

Uriah kept the stone fence on his right— between them and the ranch buildings that began to come up toward them out of the mist. When each building was in plain sight he stopped, finally, and crouched a little, staring ahead. Both his hands were spread wide atop the rock fence. There was a light showing in the main house and a brighter one glowed at the bunkhouse, but the yard was empty. Uriah drew up to his full height. His teeth were bared in satisfaction.

"Come around," he said softly. "Closer. There now. They'll be coming out to do the chores in a bit. We'll squat here behind the fence. When the first man shows . . . shoot."

Zeke scowled. "The others'll stay inside, Paw."

"Let 'em. That'll be fine. We'll torch the place. Cook 'em inside or drive 'em out." Uriah put his pink-scarred right hand on Pete Amaya's scrawny shoulder. "Slip around behind the bunkhouse, and, when the shooting's going on, fire it. You understand?"

"Yes," Amaya said, and slipped away in a hunched-over trot.

"You, Fawcett . . . watch the back of the house. They'll likely try escaping to the trees. Take someone with you."

"All right."

Uriah got down on one knee and put his rifle atop the fence. "The rest of us'll stay here." He looked around at them. "Pick your spot, boys. This is for Evans and Buell. Remember that. For Evans and Buell and Cardoza . . . and every other sheepman they've butchered in his blankets."

Lee went back along the fence behind Zeke. When they were hunkered down, waiting, he said: "Zeke, Missus Clement's in there."

"She won't get hurt."

"They've got little kids, too."

"We're only after Pax and his god-damned bushwhacking riders."

At the growl in his brother's tone Lee looked around. Zeke was bent low over his rifle. Its long barrel was bearing straight toward the ranch house. Bushy brows and one flaming green eye showed above its stock. Zeke had never looked so like Uriah before. Even the grating sound of his voice was like Uriah's. Lee touched his own

53

weapon and its coldness startled him. He faced around.

Along the fence were other guns; other heads were bent forward. There was an odd hush over everything. Someone spat tobacco juice close by and it sounded as loud as a pistol shot. Uriah's rumbling whisper passed along the line.

"No noise, now. We don't want to spoil anything."

Kant U'Ren, the half-breed from Idaho, spoke suddenly; the first words he'd said in hours. "You better pick up your spent shells," he said, without amplifying it.

They understood. They would pick up their spent casings; no lawman was going to trace them by brass dummies. Lee looked along the line for the half-breed. U'Ren was not as low behind the stones as the others and he had one boot toe dug in behind him and one shoulder braced slightly forward around his gunstock. This was nothing new to U'Ren. He had done this before, very obviously.

"It's going to rain," Zeke said, around his rifle stock. He said it so casually that Lee felt some of the tenseness leave him.

The waiting got to all of them but Uriah and, perhaps, Kant U'Ren. They fidgeted, shifted their weapons along the stones, making scraping sounds. The mist was thickening and the wind was gone. It felt a little warmer than it had back in the gully.

"Zeke?"

"Yeah."

"This isn't right. You aren't supposed to kill folks like they were sage hens."

"Folks aren't supposed to kill sheepmen like they were sage hens, either."

"This'll be plain murder, Zeke. The first man to walk out in that yard'll never know what hit him. He won't have any chance at all."

"Neither'd Lester or Carter Buell, Lee. You'd better quit thinking and just keep watch. They'll be coming out any second now."

Lee bent over his rifle. "I don't feel right about this," he mumbled.

Zeke's head lifted briefly. The green stare fastened on Lee. "You aren't the first one to say that, boy."

"What'd you mean?"

"Last night . . . when you didn't come back . . . Paw said it. Said you had no guts for fighting. Said maybe you'd shed the bodies and just kept on going."

Lee made no answer and Zeke hunched forward again. The minutes continued to pass on leaden feet. A fat drop of water struck the stones near Lee's gun. Another came down, and another. Zeke was right; it was going to rain. Looking at the drops Lee remembered Ann's tears. Then Uriah's voice interrupted his thoughts.

"There . . . watch now, boys. Someone's coming from the bunkhouse."

Lee squinted his eyes the better to see, but it was moments before he caught the thin sliver of light where a door had opened.

Guns raked softly along the fence top on his left, making a terrible sound. Hammers clicked back. Lee's sloshing heart filled his head with its sturdy pounding. He closed his eyes tightly, then opened them wide. Visibility was improved; he saw the door swinging open wider.

"To the hilt," Uriah said suddenly in a loud voice. "Give 'em steel to the hilt!"

Chapter Four

The man who came out of the bunkhouse held a kitten in his hands. He bent over to put it down. Behind him a loud voice said: "That'll learn you to leave it in here all night."

Someone fired. Lee, watching the cowboy in fascination, did not see who did it. The kitten exploded into a puff of red-stained fur and the cowboy, still bent forward, twisted his head toward the stone fence with a shocked expression. In that second more rifles sounded and at the same time the loud voice from within the bunkhouse rose in a sharp cry of startled alarm. The cowboy pitched forward off the bunkhouse stoop, slid forward on his face, and lay still.

A second man, shirtless and barefoot, sprang through the doorway. His face was twisted ugly and a pistol rode high in one hand. Along the fence row a second volley rang out. The cowboy was hurled against the bunkhouse wall. His pistol exploded, plowing a long furrow at his feet. His knees sprung outward and he fell.

Within the bunkhouse Clement's third rider snuffed out the lamp and slammed the door. As far away as Lee was, he heard the bar drop into place behind it.

He wasn't conscious of standing fully upright until Zeke said: "Get down, you fool! There's still one in there!"

Uriah roared it, too. "Down! Down, boys! Wait for the flames!"

Silence did not come into the yard right away. There was the echo, the reverberations, and, before they died away, a man's keening voice in sharp surprise from the main house, then silence. A long hollow hush broken only by the grating of booted feet behind the rock fence, the sniffling of a few men, the raking of their guns along the topmost rocks.

"You never fired," Zeke said as Lee looked around at him. "You stood there with your mouth hanging open."

Lee didn't answer. He drew down lower, looking out where the mist swirled and soft raindrops fell.

"Smoke," someone said. "Yonder by the bunk-house."

Uriah's unmistakable voice came next. "Watch sharp now, boys. He'll be coming out soon."

Clement's bunkhouse was old and tinder dry. It burned well. The heat quivered outward as far as the fence. It felt good against those tight faces there. Smoke eddied out where mud chinking had crumbled. The man inside could not stand it much longer.

Pete Amaya came back to them in the same low-crouching run he'd used to go light the fire. His teeth shone and his dark eyes flashed with cruel pleasure. Lee had only a glimpse of him as he darted past, heading down where Uriah was.

"There!" Zeke said, and fired.

Lee swung forward in time to see the cowboy make his attempt. He was already past the door, beyond the porch, over the two bodies, and zigzagging toward the main house. Uriah's explosive shout came loud and ringing.

"To the hilt, boys! To the hilt!"

Guns flamed. Gray dust jerked to life around the sprinting figure. The cowboy staggered, sagged, then took two more steps and crumpled low. As soon as he was down Uriah hurdled the fence and brandished his rifle.

"Come on, boys . . . at 'em! To the house!"

Lee had a glimpse of his wide-open mouth. He caught the flush of dark color in his father's face and the burning ferocity in his eyes, then Zeke was yelling something at him. They all followed

Uriah over the fence in a wild run toward the house. Smoke and flames both spiraled upward from the ravished bunkhouse. Red shadows danced across the front of Paxton Clement's home as the sheepmen swarmed up under the low overhang close upon Uriah's heels. When they stopped, Kant U'Ren was panting beside Lee. He turned his head heavily and made a mirthless, silent smile.

Uriah stood a moment listening, then he rapped twice on the log wall, hard, with the butt of his rifle. The sound rang hollow in the stillness, and a quiet followed. Again he rapped and this time there was answering sound, the sliding of steel over wood. They knew that noise and scattered hastily, several making little cries of warning. Someone inside was pushing a rifle through a loophole.

The strain was intense. Somewhere a long way off a dog was frenziedly barking. Until that moment Lee had forgotten that Paxton Clement had a dog. Evidently the first firing had frightened the animal off.

"Is that you, Gorman?" a thick voice demanded through the log wall.

"It's me, Clement. Come out of there."

"You come and get me . . . you damned murderer."

Where they were flattened along the wall, Lee's companions were holding their breath, listening.

Only Uriah stood away from the mud wattle a short distance, holding his rifle in both hands, his head thrown back, and his face red-stained by exertion and firelight. In that moment he looked more than ever like one of the old-time prophets with his hair tumbled and his beard awry, and sealed judgment immutable in the expression of his face.

"Look at that bunkhouse, Clement. This house'll burn just as quick."

Silence again, broken only by crackling flames. Zeke, with his head pressed flat against the wall, said: "They're talking in there. I hear someone crying."

Uriah nodded. "Clement! Come out and the young 'uns won't be hurt. If we have to burn you out, I won't promise nothing."

Another interval of silence, then a woman screamed and over that unnerving sound there was a crash of furniture.

Uriah spun half around. "Zeke! Take Pete and Lee and go around back. If he comes out, shoot him."

Lee trotted after his brother and grinning Pete Amaya followed them both. Behind the house the dog's distant barking sounded louder. Amaya put his lips close to Lee's ear.

"He's got a golden-haired daughter in there, *compadre*."

"Shut up!" Zeke hissed.

Amaya slunk back and squatted down to watch. It was a brief and fruitless vigil. Gaspar Pompa came up excitedly and told them: "He open the door. Uriah got him around front."

They stumped back through the rain-dappled dust where the others were crowding inside the house. From far back Lee could see over the other heads. Paxton Clement, shorter than Uriah, was backing across the room. There was no fear in his expression but his forehead was white and glistening. Behind a flung-back sacking curtain was a wide bed. From the farther side of it an elderly woman watched. She was swathed in rumpled bedclothes and her sleep-puffy face was coarse and ugly to look at. The fourteen men crowding into the room with gleaming guns were fearful to see. She made whimpering sounds deep in her throat.

Paxton Clement had on boots and trousers. His underwear showed where his shirt might have been; it was soiled and worn.

"Come outside," Uriah said harshly, looking down straight into the cowman's grizzled face.

"No," the woman said thinly. "No. You can't take him." She was writhing in the bed, holding the covers around her with clenched hands. "You haven't got the right. You get out of here."

"Be still," Uriah said with an urgent ringing in his voice.

Lee saw movement in a far corner. A tall blonde

girl in a soiled wrapper and a boy no more than twelve years old were there. The boy was clinging to the tall girl who moved forward now. Her eyes were wide with fright and her full-lipped mouth was a red scar in the paleness of her face. "Get out of here!" she screamed at them. "Get out, get out, get out!"

George Fawcett moved toward her. His shoulders were braced forward. Lee could see only his back and the way he held his gun up across his body as though to push the girl and boy with it.

Uriah ignored everyone but Paxton Clement. "Walk out or get drug out," he said with dull fire.

Clement stared in total silence, motionless but also without fear. The woman began to wail. She stormed in the bed, keeping the covers about her. Her bleating was the only sound in the candle-lit room until Uriah put forth his hand to grasp Clement. Then the cowman found his voice. He swore at them with his legs planted widely and his hands knotted into fists, then jerked away from Uriah's touch and cursed them savagely.

Beside Lee and slightly in front, Kant U'Ren made his mirthless, wordless smile again and slouched against the wall, waiting. Uriah's hand dropped to his side. He moved aside and gestured for the others to do the same. There was an open lane between the sheepmen and the fire-lit yard beyond, where a cooling body lay halfway between the main house and bunkhouse. Uriah raised his arm, pointing. He was white to the lips from Clement's cursing. For only a moment longer did Paxton Clement remain still. Then he started forward toward the yard and behind his sharply drawn shoulders and straight back the woman was crying: "No, no, no, no, no . . . !"

When Clement passed the youngest Gorman at the doorway, Lee saw in his face not the terror that should have been there, not fear or even desperation, only the terrible bitterness of a man who believed what was happening to him should be happening instead to his captors.

Lee moved out into the gusty heat of the yard with the others. Back by the door four men stood blocking the opening against the shrieking, gibbering girl, her brother, and their mother, whose screams rose keenly over the rattle of falling timbers and bursting flames from the bunkhouse.

Lee was rooted. Bulking shadows closed in around Clement where he stopped, looking down at his dead rider.

"Don't, Paw. For Christ's sake what are you doing?"

"Be still," Zeke said, at Lee's side. The others had not heard, but Zeke, coming up close, had caught each word. Now he stopped and Lee saw the iron set of his jaw and the bloodless straining of his mouth. "He's got it coming."

Uriah was talking again, his voice flat-sounding

and scornfully cold. Red light flickered over them all and out beyond, where earth and sky merged in dawn's sickly light, lay a sea of grayness.

"You started it, Clement. You kept them at it. You led their night riders. If you want to make your peace, make it."

Clement, shorter than most of them, looked up unflinchingly. He glared into each face before he said: "You god-damned bastards! You sheep-stinkin' scum! D'you think you'll get away with this . . . ?"

"You'd better quit cussing and pray," Uriah said, stepping back and raising his rifle to hip-height, cocking it, and curling one pink-scarred finger around the cold trigger.

Clement twisted his face into a bitter grimace. "Pray? You'd like to see me get down and pray, wouldn't you, Gorman . . . you filthy Secesh scum? Well, shoot and be damned to you . . . every one of you'll hang for this. Every one!"

Uriah fired first, from a distance of less than ten feet. Clement spun half around. Then the others fired and Clement staggered in agony but he did not go down quickly. His underwear reddened as he swayed. Then Pete Amaya leaped forward nimbly, put a revolver against the dying man's head, and pressed the trigger. There was a sound of breaking bone, of tearing flesh, and Paxton Clement's eyes bulged crazily and he broke over backward.

They stood above him unaware of the wild shrieks beyond the blocked door of the house, looking down. Blood as black as ink oozed out over the yard, a shiny red from the firelight.

"Come on," Uriah said finally, turning away. "There's no time to lose."

Kant U'Ren spoke up. "What about the kid and girl and the old woman?"

Uriah stopped in his tracks looking around. "What about 'em?"

"They're witnesses. They can hang every damned one of us."

Uriah was shaking his head before U'Ren finished. "No, they saw nothing. The only witness to who shot Clement is lying back there with half his damned head blown off. Now come on . . . and hurry."

He led them back along the stone fence through a falling drizzle that was growing stronger all the time, back through the timber to the erosion slash and to their horses. There, as they were fumbling anxiously with their mounts, he spoke again, from the saddle.

"Every one of you go back to your camps. Clean your guns, turn out your horses, and eat breakfast. When the law comes, remember that you haven't seen any of the others since the time we met before this. You know nothing about Clement's death. Blot this morning out of your memories." He shortened his reins. "One more thing. You may be arrested . . . don't resist. They won't be able to hold you long and the rest of us'll fight to help you. Now then, they'll likely take me first. If they do . . . Zeke'll take my place as your leader. Do what he says. . . . Now ride!"

They left the gully with an increasing rain making the ground underfoot treacherously slippery. The first one to break off was Kant U'Ren. He left them while they were still in the trees. The next to go was Pete Amaya. He was followed by Gaspar Pompa and George Fawcett. By the time the plateau was in view through the drenching water only Lee and Zeke were riding with Uriah.

Uriah off-saddled, motioned the horse away, and dragged his tack under the canvas lean-to behind their camp wagon. There, he spread the saddle blanket to dry and sat down to clean his rifle. He neither looked at nor spoke to his sons.

Zeke built a small fire in clamp-jawed silence just beyond the lean-to's opening. When it was blazing bright and sending forth heat, he went back into the shadows to clean his gun. From time to time he looked out where Lee was unsaddling with numb fingers. He had his gun wiped clear of tell-tale stains and smell when the younger man came in under the shelter. Zeke got the black coffee pot, filled it, and put it over the fire. He laid out three tin cups, put rye whiskey into two of them with a grudging measure but poured generously into the third cup, then, when the coffee was hot, he filled each cup to the brim. Uriah got one cup; he nodded and put it aside. Zeke kept the second cup and Lee got the one that was nearly half rye whiskey. He drank it without a pause; water poured into his eyes; he coughed and spat and sat down, cross-legged, to clean the rifle he had not fired.

The rain continued steadily and monotonously. Zeke's fire sizzled and its orange flames showed brightly in under the lean-to's dripping cover. Uriah sat like stone, gazing outward over the drowning land. His profile, bearded and Pharaoh-like, was sharply chiseled. Every plane and angle stood out clear to see. Zeke refilled the tin cup and drank deeply. His gaze rarely left Lee's bowed shoulders. Finally Uriah drew up and looked around him. It was as though he was emerging from a trance. He cleared his throat and spat, then he stood up, raw-boned and hard-cut in the wavering light.

"I'm going to the creek," he said dully, and moved off.

The rainfall was like distant drumming. Through its constant roar came the occasional bleat of sheep. Zeke tossed the tin cup aside, pushed long legs far out, and spoke. "That's only the beginning," he said, watching Lee's shoulders quicken with movement at the sound of his voice. "There'll be more. They got in their licks first, then we got in ours . . . now it's their turn again."

"But, Zeke . . . not in cold blood," the bowed head said in a muffled way. "Not like they're varmints."

"Make you a little sick, did it, boy?"

Lee's head rose and fell. Behind him Zeke wore a curious expression. He could remember the strong feeling they'd had between them as children; it had been strongest in the moments when their father had seemed the most remote to them. It had never atrophied, that feeling. Zeke understood his brother. Knew him far better than the old man did and probably better than their mother had. But they were men now and they were committed to Uriah's ways.

Zeke looked at the tin cup for a moment, then gathered in his legs and got up, taking the cup to the jug and sloshing whiskey into it. "Here," he said, thrusting it over Lee's shoulder. "Drink it down."

Lee did not turn or take the cup. He heard Zeke's teeth strike the tin. He heard him swallowing. Then he felt him hunkering close and saw his big arm go out to stir the sputtering fire.

"Boy, I'll tell you what. You saddle up and go see Ann."

Lee looked around, then.

"Sure, go on. I'll tell Paw you've gone looking for strays." Zeke made a slightly drunken gesture. " 'S'all right. I can handle him. Saddle up and go see Ann." Zeke's green eyes were dark-ringed and cloudy-looking. "Someone in this god-damned family ought t'have a woman. A decent honest true woman. It's never going to be me . . . I can tell you that right now." His lips pulled up in a bleak grin. "It's sure Lord not going t'be Paw." He croaked a hard laugh. "Can you picture the old man with a woman . . . ? Holy hell!" The harsh laugh grew louder for a moment, then stopped short. "Go on, Lee. Go see Ann. Get the poison out of you with her. Come back when you're good and ready." Zeke's huge hand moved swiftly, caught Lee in an iron grip, and gave him a savage shove. "Go on, damn you!"

Lee went. He saddled up and rode down through the rain and he hadn't covered a quarter mile before the black poncho he wore was shiny with water. Once, far out, he looked back. The plateau was dimly discernible but neither his brother's hulking figure nor the little fire was visible. He pushed on, and behind him the world faded into slate-gray opaqueness. Everything was blotted out—the bodies, the burning bunkhouse, the keening shrieks that were the last echoes to leave his mind, and finally his recollection of Uriah sitting there behind the fire under the lean-to, staring outward farther than anyone could hope to see.

Chapter Five

Where he crossed Cottonwood Creek was a shoal, but even so his horse had to brace against the pulsing might of a heavily heaving current, swollen now and chocolate-brown.

A spiral of bluish smoke rose straight up beyond a long swell of land between the creek and the Foster place. Lee rode toward it. When he topped out over the rise, the Foster place was huddled in a millrace of mud and water below. His horse was reluctant to descend and when forced to do so he placed each hoof well down before moving the next one. They only slipped once, and that was where the land flattened out not far from the rough-hewn log barn.

He rode in and instantly saw the bending figure below a smoking lantern near the hen roost. The fullness was familiar; the wealth of tumbled black hair shone obsidian-like with raindrops.

"Ann?"

She turned and straightened up slowly. "Lee . . ." Both hands were full of eggs. "Whatever are you doing riding out on a day like this?"

He dismounted, led his horse to a tie stall, and made it fast to a manger of grass hay before he turned back to face her. She had put the eggs into a basket and had moved across to where he was.

"I had to see you."

She waited, saying nothing. There was a strong pulse beating in her throat. Her tilted face was as clear as marble in the barn's gloom.

He moved away from the horse, shook his head, and flicked water from nose and chin. "I just had to see you again is all. . . ."

She continued her silence, staring into his eyes. Hot blood ran into his neck and stained his cheeks. He fought against looking away from her. His voice grew rough edged.

"Well, shouldn't I have . . . Ann?"

"Take your slicker off, Lee."

He obeyed. Beneath, his clothing was dry. For a second he thought he smelled a residue of smoke rising from his shirt and pants. Then he forgot again when she had her head against his breast, her arms tightly wound around him, and the full length of her pressing into him burning like fire.

"I knew you'd come," she said, low and husky. "You had to . . . I knew you would."

"Your paw might come out. . . ."

"No. Some fellers came by a while back and he rode off with them."

She released him and stepped back. There were tears in her eyes and her lips were trembling. She seemed to be balancing a thought in her mind. Then she said: "Up in the loft. Come on."

He followed her hand over hand up the pole ladder to where a heavy grass hay fragrance filled his nostrils. She kicked at the hay, making places, then sank down and drew him down beside her. For a moment longer the ecstatic look lingered, then, seeing his dulled expression, her face changed. The expression went flat, almost ugly, before it altered finally into a set, bitter small smile and she lay back with her head propped on one hand. Wisdom as old as time itself was in her eyes, intuitive female wisdom.

"I know why you came, Lee."

He heard the huskiness, saw the steady kindling hotness in her face, and would have shook his head at it because that was not basically why he had come at all. But she put out one hand, touched his flesh with her fingers, and his ears roared. He reached for her. There was a sob in his throat for the unresolved conflicts inside his head. She responded with an abandon that left him without breath.

She kissed his face, his throat, his mouth, in a tempest of agony and tenderness. Her jet hair fell across him and her hands went under his shirt.

"I love you, Lee. You know that. But you don't know how much I love you."

"Ann . . ."

A wetness came to his eyes. A tear ran under his lashes. His head rocked slowly from side to side until her damp palms held it, then his body went loose and languor came. He did not know whether he was awake or asleep but he knew he was exhausted, that his body was loose in every joint and muscle and if he'd had to leap up suddenly to save his life, he couldn't have.

She lay there beside him with his right hand on her breast. The heartbeats were uneven and sledge-like. They jarred her entire body.

"Ann . . . we killed Paxton Clement this morning."

"What?"

He told her, his voice liquid-soft, words flowing in cadence to the diminishing power of the storm outside. She raised up and his hand fell away. She was staring down at him with her eyes suddenly enormous and her full lips lying open and slack.

"Lee!"

The wrenched-out, stunned, and thick way she said his name did not alleviate his breathless condition. He continued to lie there motionlessly with his eyes tightly closed and his head filled with the slackening beat of raindrops overhead. Then she was moving briskly in the hay, kicking it away from her. When next she spoke all trace of passion was gone.

"Get up, Lee."

He opened his eyes. She was standing over him, big-eyed and ashen.

"Get up!"

He stirred, pushed up on his elbows, and continued to stare at her.

"Those men Paw rode off with . . . when they came up, they called him out. They talked for a spell, and then he got his gun and a horse and raced off with them. Don't you understand . . . now?"

He should understand, he knew, but his mind was lethargic. Like Sampson he had been shorn. He was as weak now as a cat.

She caught at him, dragged him upright. "I'll go make us a bundle. You saddle another horse and wait for me." Her hands moved agitatedly across his rumpled shirt front. "Hurry!"

He watched her hasten down the pole ladder, heard the solid footfalls as she left the barn. Then he moved, also, but more slowly and ponderously. He found a saddle and a chunky bay mare. While he worked, strength began to return. By the time she was back—with an oversize wool Mackinaw around her—he had the horses ready. She shot him only a brief stare, then grabbed at the mare's reins and started for the barn's rear doorway afoot. He followed.

"Stay close!" she called, and he moved faster.

They went like phantoms, he with a great shambling gait that was half walk, half trot, she with the strong power of her fear, darkly, silently enduring, stoically suffering from want of air and with a strange giddiness in her head, but never slowing until they were part way up the land swell, well away from the barn. Then she stopped and gazed backward. He heard the sob catch in her throat. The rain had stopped altogether now. There remained only dismal grayness and a misty drizzle. The day was warm. He, too, looked back. The house of her parents and the rough-hewn barn looked unreal with mist swirling around them. The air revived him fully. His hands grew hot with sweat and the sourness of his agitation made the horses roll their eyes, snort, and bunch up.

"Let's ride," she said, and sprang up.

He watched her mount with a hardness in his throat, then he mounted and pushed up beside her. They breasted the hill and he took the lead—westward.

"No," she said. "The other way. South!"

His face swung toward her in blurred softness. "Ann, I can't . . . I can't run off and leave Zeke and the old man to face things alone."

Nor would argument sway him. Desperation poured out of her until she caught the acidity of his profile, then she became silent.

After a time he turned toward her. "I want you to understand, Ann. I never knew anybody before that I thought would understand."

There was a blind allegiance in his look that stilled her. Dammed behind her teeth were words of desperation that rang like flutes in her mind. *Why must he be so weak? Why must his paw have such an iron hold on him?*

"You understand . . . ?"

"I understand," she replied, fighting nausea. "I understand a lot better than you do, Lee. I love you . . . I'm willing to run away with you . . . unmarried even. And you're taking me back to that sheep camp."

"No, Ann, we'll go." There grew a softness in his voice. "We'll have things right . . . you'll see."

Cottonwood Creek came up out of the mist. It was over its banks and rumbling in full throat. He reined up. Her troubled eyes, shades darker than usual, followed its southward twisting a moment before she spoke.

"We'll have to go to the narrows. Maybe we can cross there."

They swung south paralleling the twisted and quivering willow breaks, tall and swaying in the murk. Beyond, through the sedge they could see the creek all dark and oily with a pale miasmic cloudiness above it.

Heaven broke up in mottled spots and beyond, farther out, was clean blue sky. The storm had passed; in time the sun would come. Underfoot the ground steamed. Their horses, passing over it, made the only sound excepting the low hissing of the creek. The hours slipped by.

Lee rode ahead in a brooding way, his face sad and wistful-looking. He swayed with the saddle, lost among a tumbling bramble of thoughts. Then the sun came out, a gigantic smoldering disc of it all, pale and swollen. Heat came, too, oppressive heat full of earth scent and humidity.

It was Ann who broke the long silence. She

drew up, pointing downward. "There . . . fresh tracks, Lee."

He looked. Around each shod-horse imprint dark soil was crumbling. "Can't be very old," he said.

"Nor very far ahead. Now will you branch off?"

"I can't."

She followed after when he pushed on. They did not stop again until he saw a faint twisting of horsemen far ahead, off to their right near higher ground.

"Riders, Ann."

"Yes."

Her voice was toneless and her gaze, like his, was fixed on distant movement. She trembled and he saw it.

"What's the matter?"

"I don't know. Fright I reckon."

"Could they be the men with your paw?"

"I hope not. I don't know. It's too far. . . ."

"Who were they, Ann?"

"Cowmen," she replied in the same toneless way. "Charley Simpson . . . Dade . . . I didn't pay much attention. There were about eight of them." Her gaze returned to his face. "Then it didn't matter . . . I didn't care. Lee?"

"Yes."

"The creek's been turning easterly for the last hour or so. The farther we follow it the closer it'll take us to Union City. Listen to me. There's nothing but cattlemen on this side. Please, Lee . . . let's swim it and keep going south. Please . . ."

He continued to gaze where the horsemen had vanished into a thin stand of second-growth pine. "It might be Indians," he mused, ignoring her plea. It was the first time in his life the notion of Indians was a relief to his mind.

She dashed the hope: "On shod horses?"

He gathered the reins without looking at her. "Ride down in here," he said, and urged his reluctant mount in among water-lapped willows. "Less chance they'll see us."

They wound among the willows with branches stinging their faces until the fetid heat and the difficulty their animals had holding footing drove them back out again.

"Wait here," said Lee. "I'll take another look."

"We'll both look." She rode past him out into the open so that he had no chance to argue.

The land sloped gently away from them toward distant lifts and rises. Sparkling sunlight reflected from each south slope with hurting brilliance. He stood in his stirrups, catching movement again. "Looks like they're cutting down in front of us, Ann."

"Where? Can you see them?"

"Yonder. Up that timbered side hill to the left." He dropped down. "I'll go closer. If they keep on, they'll cut us off."

Without speaking, she kept her horse even with

his as they moved carefully forward. While he was squinting ahead, she cast a careless glance over her shoulder—and a gust of breath burst from her. He turned quickly struck by this instinctive sound of alarm.

"What? What is it?"

"Look back there. It's more riders, Lee. Behind us. Coming along the creek . . . like they're tracking. . . ."

He was galvanized to action. While his horse spun away from the creek, he called to her: "Come on . . . back up the creek, then make for those trees on the bluff!"

As they loped down their back trail, he twisted from time to time for a backward look, and finally there was terror in him. They could not escape. As soon as they broke cover and made for the timber, they would be seen. Fear choked him. His body grew oily under its clothing. The same horror must have touched Ann because suddenly she drew up.

"Come on!" he called, slowing.

"They'll see us, Lee!"

"No matter now . . . we can't stay here."

"Lee wait. Please wait . . ."

He yanked back, staring at her. She was watching the distant riders. Her face had gone deathly pale and she was biting her underlip as though in pain.

"Ann," he cried out desperately, "you want to

see me hung? Look how they're working the willows, riding slow and all. They're after us." Impatience made him reach for her reins. "Come on!"

She booted the chunky mare out behind him. For a short distance they rode stirrup-to-stirrup. Over the dull smash of hoofs on sodden earth she cried: "It *can't* be a posse, Lee, how could they be here so fast?"

"Right now I don't care how," he answered from ashen lips. "If we can make those trees, we stand a chance."

They whirled clear of the willows and struck out in a belly-down run. At that moment someone fired a pistol. Lee swiveled in his saddle. The men who had been tracking them were dismounting where the tracks went into the water. The pistol shot had been a signal for the larger body of riders to come up. They were turning back from their bisecting angle toward the creek when the fugitives broke out of the willows. Instantly Lee saw men flourish carbines and jump out their horses. They had been seen.

"Lee . . . !"

"I see. Ride for it!"

They rode hard but in that muggy heat a horse could not endure the pace long and they had to slow long before the trees could be reached. They alternated between a slamming gallop and an even more agonized trot. Just as the trees came up close, Lee made a long sweep of the land behind them. The trackers were no longer in sight but the larger party of riders was after them in full throat. Even as he watched, one horse went end over end in the treacherous mud, throwing his rider like a pinwheel through the air. The others did not stop.

They got into the trees only to discover there was no succor there; the sparsest kind of timber grew only atop the ridge. Beyond was open country again, spotted now and then by brush clumps. Lee did not look back again. This was unknown land to him. He concentrated on picking their course, hoping that by bending south he could by-pass the large body of posse men.

"Lee!"

He looked around. Ann was gasping; her face was beaded with sweat and her eyes were closed so tightly that water had been squeezed out around them. He slowed.

"What is it?"

"I'm sick."

"Oh, God, you can't be."

"You keep going," she said with her eyes closed, clinging to the saddle horn, and going lower with each slamming jar of her racing horse.

He drew back and closed in, put out a hand to steady her. They rode down the steaming land that way with the lemon-yellow sun overhead. It slowed them considerably and coming on behind them, larger now, were the men from the creek.

Horses fresher and running hard. She began to slip sideways. He could not right her until they stopped. A fierce push set her back astraddle.

Still with her eyes pinched closed she said: "Keep going, Lee." The words were nearly throttled by locked jaws. "Just keep going. Please, Lee . . ."

"I don't want to leave you, Ann."

"They don't want . . . me. Go on, Lee. Hurry!" Her eyes flew open, swimming in agony and half rational.

"No," he said sharply, and led her horse in the gradual descent back toward the creek, senseless to the fact that he was making straight for the larger band of riders.

Far ahead he saw something shimmering and thought it might be some form of hope. Then the shimmering turned to a many-spiked gleam of sunlight off metal, and consciousness warned him it was armed men riding with their guns naked and upraised. He was trying to clear his mind of cloudiness when the chunky mare stumbled. He looked around just in time to see Ann fall, to hear her body strike hard with a soggy thump.

He leaped down, holding both their reins. "Ann! Ann! For God's sake get up." He slapped her face. Sweat fell from his chin onto her blouse, staining it with darkness. "Ann . . . !"

A distant strident yell came softly.

He struggled upright and faced them. They were

coming from both directions and the sharp glitter of guns was like silver. The long cry was repeated. They were slowing now, coming toward him steadily, and although they did not know why he was standing there above the crumpled form in the mud, you could see in the way they rode, straight up and wire tight, that they were savoring grim victory.

"Lee . . . please go on."

She was gazing straight up into his face from the shade of his big right leg, wide-planted. Her underlip was bleeding where she'd bitten through it.

"No!"

"You must. You've got to."

He kneeled swiftly with his back to the line of horsemen fanning out. "I'll carry you."

He got his arms under her, heaved upright, and although she was strangely light against the massive bunching of his muscles, his heart beat nigh to bursting. She stared into his face and a great welter of tears broke and ran down her cheeks.

Some way he got back into the saddle and kicked the beast forward in a shambling trot. The chunky mare tagged along, reins dragging in the mud. There was complete futility to it and even in her semi-conscious condition Ann knew it, even if he refused to accept it.

He was well within carbine range now and the

flatness of a gunshot brought him back to reason. The riders were coming up fast in front and behind, and his horse was laboring heavily. He stumbled, too, frequently, and sucked in air like wind whistling through a too-small hole. The man looked at the burden in his arms. He saw the heroic staunchness of her in his dimming heart and choked over words that rasped in his throat. The horse fell heavily almost with a sigh and it was over.

He sat in the mud, cradling her head in his lap. There was blood running from his left ear; its stickiness ran under his collar and mingled with sweat.

The first rider to come up yanked back with one hand and leveled a Dragoon pistol with the other. His face was burned red-brown around a graceful sweep of curling moustache.

"Get up, damn you! Stand up!"

"I can't."

The big pistol wavered. Other riders came plodding up, staring downward.

"Are you hurt?"

"No." He touched Ann's face with muddy fingers. "She is."

"Leave her be and stand up!"

They swung down and scattered out around him, their faces flushed and hard. He recognized several of them. He put her head down gently and stood upright.

The other riders were now approaching. A man said: "Plenty of trees back up the ridge." Others echoed approval and a heated discussion ensued during which the second band of horsemen came up and dismounted. Lee saw Charley Simpson's granite face among them. Near him was his moon-faced son Dade Simpson. Farther back was Lew Foster, Ann's father. He was pushing through the bunched-up mob.

A second man shouldering past, Lee recognized at once. He was the Union City town marshal, Bob Ander. He wore a rusty black hat and his little eyes were hidden behind folds of perpetually puckered flesh.

"Where are the others?" he demanded of Lee.

"What others?"

"Your paw . . . your brother . . . the others who raided XIH this morning. Where are they?"

"I don't know. I guess maybe they . . ."

"Yes, you do. You know all right. You wasn't trying to escape by yourself. Where are they?"

Someone cried out: "Hang the murderin' devil!" Another voice said: "Better'n that . . . shoot him right here."

"Shut up!" Ander ordered in a lashing tone. "Boy, you'd better tell. You split off from 'em, didn't you? Where did they go?"

"No, I didn't split off from them. I don't know where they are. I'm not lying."

Lew Foster broke through the last rank of posse

men, saw his daughter lying at Lee Gorman's feet, and gave a sharp cry and a forward lurch. He dropped down and gathered the girl against him. Marshal Ander and the others, temporarily averted, looked down.

"What's wrong with her, Lew?" someone asked quietly. An older man, unfamiliar to Lee, edged up and hunkered down, squinting at Ann's face in her father's arms.

Lee lowered his head, also. "She said she was sick."

The quiet elderly man got back upright stiffly and looked closely at Lee.

Behind Bob Ander a rough voice spoke out: "Let's take him back to the oaks. Catching one's better'n catching none."

Bob Ander swore at them again, but it was the quiet stranger's voice and words that finally brought silence. It was the dead-calm tone that made his tidings all the heavier. He spoke like a man who had abandoned ferocity in the face of something too massive to be overcome with anger.

"Yeah, hang him . . . and what'll you do with her . . . leave her and her young 'un? Leave her to watch him kick his life away and mark the child?"

There was a sucked-back silence. From the mud beside Lee Gorman, Lew Foster raised his head slowly. He was as white as death; his eyes were twisted in bulging disbelief.

"Matt," he croaked, "what the hell are you talking about?"

"Your girl," the elderly man said gently. "Remember I raised five daughters, Lew. I seen 'em all married, too. You think I don't know what ails 'em at a time like this? She's with child, Lew."

Chapter Six

They took Lee to Union City and jailed him. He did not know what had become of Ann, and when he asked, instead of answers, he got back bleak stares and threatening silence. There was much talk of lynching him. Town Marshal Ander wired the U.S. marshal's office down in Denver for help. He had his reply. Burt Garner was on his way back to Wyoming Territory.

Lee was locked in a stone room with an iron door and two padlocks. There was a twenty-four-hour guard outside and only Bob Ander could visit him. But Ander did not come, so Lee languished, desperately afraid and lonely, until the night of June 3rd, a hot, still night without a moon and overcast, oppressively hushed and humid. Then Uriah came.

Zeke was with them. It was Zeke who clubbed down the guard. Shadowy in the middle distance were others—Kant U'Ren, Pete Amaya, Joseph Fawcett, Gaspar Pompa—thirteen of them bristling with knives and guns.

It was a well-planned raid. It was carried off in absolute silence and with split-second timing. Uriah knew how such things were done. He had made no move toward Union City for six long days. It had been necessary for much of the excitement to die away first. Then he had come, leading the others, wraith-like and vengeful, his strange eyes bright with danger and his bloodless slit of a mouth curled in hard triumph.

Nothing went wrong. They had Lee out and on a horse within fifteen minutes of the time they had followed a failing moon into Union City. They left town, not in a run but in a slow and silent walk. The villagers slumbered peacefully around them. They rode far out before Uriah flapped his arms and kicked his mount into a long lope, then they made haste back to the mountains. There, Lee discovered, they had a secret camp cached in the furry crotch of two sentinel hills. There, he got down and watched the others care for their animals, then head for an iron stew pot that was suspended above a smoldering pit between two logs. Zeke came up beside him; he looked older than when last they'd talked. Older and dirtier and tired.

"He's going to read you the Articles of War," Zeke said. They both knew who he meant. "He's been raging ever since Lew Foster come to the plateau." Zeke spat and did not bring his gaze back to his brother's face. "Foster was out to kill you . . . except he couldn't. They had you in jail. Paw didn't believe him at first . . . then he did. . . . Well, come on. Might as well face him and get it over with."

They went toward the others, side-by-side, big men, long of stride and corded with muscle. The others looked at them and at Uriah. Uriah had not spoken since they had left Union City. His face was stone-set now and savage-looking. His eyes seemed hotter and dryer than Lee had ever seen them look before, when they focused on him.

"Sit down," Uriah commanded, ignoring Zeke and the others. Then for a long interval he did not open his lips again.

"Wallowing on a mud bank like a cub bear," he said finally in a low-burning and scornful voice, and every word carried. Where the others sat, heads down and bodies motionless, it was obvious they were listening with relish. Not a one of them but had felt the lash of Uriah's wrath some time. It was good now to hear him flay someone else, especially his son.

"Rolling in the weeds with Lew Foster's girl . . . Sneaking away after the raid like a scared whelp dog . . . Getting caught and making us all risk our hides to fetch you clear again . . ."

"Paw . . ."

"Shut up, Zeke, I'll handle this.

"Running out on us when you knew the cowmen'd strike back." Uriah drew up and looked fully at Lee, his strange eyes boring in fiercely. "What kind of man are you anyway? We got a war on our hands . . . a fighting war . . . and you go skulking off to lie with that girl!"

Lee was like rock. The tongue that was cloven to the roof of his mouth was as wood. His eyes burned and big-fisted hands lay still in his lap. He did not meet his father's glare.

Zeke pushed between them with a cup of laced coffee for his brother. Silence settled heavily. Zeke's massiveness effectively cut Lee off from Uriah's embittered stare. Later, after Uriah had flung away with an oath, Zeke took his brother to the farthest limits of the fire-lit bivouac, and there they sat hunched over on a deadfall tree, each with his tin mug of rye whiskey and coffee.

"Like I told you," said Zeke dully. "If she come up calvy, there'd be trouble. That's partly what's eating at Paw."

"Why should it bother him . . . it's my worry not his."

"He sort of figured we could get some of the squatters to throw in with us against the big outfits."

"Well, what's Ann got to do with that?" Lee wanted to know.

Big Zeke had both hands cupped around the tin mug, warming them. "Lew Foster," he said quietly. "He's joined with the big outfits. He's a power among the squatters. He'll take most of 'em into the other camp now." Zeke drained the cup and sat up straighter. "Boy, you sure kicked a skunk this time."

"Zeke?"

"Oh, hell, don't fret too much," the older brother growled gently, looking over where the others were eating and sprawling. "The old man'll get over it . . . this god-damned world keeps on turning, seems like . . ." He stretched.

"But what are you all doing here? Why isn't everyone at the camps? Who's watching the bands?"

"The bands," Zeke replied shortly, "are all herded together. Things've happened since they caught you, boy. They came into the hills about thirty strong . . . caught a couple of those immigrant herders and killed them. Then they raided the plateau . . . burned our wagon, wrecked the camp, and shot sheep till they ran out of bullets. We were over at Pompa's the day they came."

"Who's leading them now?"

"The Simpsons. Old Charley and young Dade. They keep watchers on the hilltops. They know we're in the hills somewhere but they don't know where." Zeke dropped the empty tin cup. "They put up posters around the country . . . we're outlaws now."

Lee looked down where the others were lolling near the dying embers. Tobacco smoke rose.

There was a little desultory talk but mostly the men lay back looking into the fire or above, at the paling sky of dawn.

"What's Paw going to do?"

"We're going to Bethel today," Zeke replied. "This is like the war all over again to him. He says we got to have a base for supplies. That's why we're going to Bethel. For supplies and more men . . . if we can get 'em." Zeke stretched again and turned his head toward Lee's profile. "The story we got . . . Lew Foster's girl was with you when they ran you down. Tell me about it."

"We were running away . . . I guess. The two of us."

"You guess . . . don't you know whether you were running away or not?"

"We had to go south, Zeke. The creek was way too high to ford. We were following it south . . . but it kept bearing toward Union City. I wanted to come back. Ann said for us to break away and keep going south. I was wondering what to do . . . exactly . . . when they came on to us." The younger man shook his head. "I don't know which I'd have done, Zeke. . . . At first I wanted to go back to the plateau, but later . . . I don't know."

A stalking shadow went past, leading a saddled horse. It was Uriah. He led his beast up to the fire and stood there, saying nothing. The others got up wearily and moved off to get their horses. Scarcely a word was spoken.

Zeke stood up, watched the bustle a moment, then brushed fingers across his brother's shoulder. "Come on, boy, we're Bethel bound."

They rode gaunt animals through the pearl-gray dawn. It was warm and still with a long streak of pink across the underbelly of sky along the farthest mountains to the east. There was neither moon nor sun. It was the between hour—the best time for fugitives to ride. Visibility was in their favor. They could see without being seen. Uriah knew these things. They followed the dim roads, a ragged line of men going by twos. Where dwellings lay they detoured wide and several times dismounted to lead their horses furtively through the gloom. When the hills were far behind and the open country stretched ahead, they gave rein and spur, fleeing over the range in a swift mass, and finally, with the village of Bethel in sight, Uriah made for a forested spit and drew up there, looking out.

Dawn was spreading. A pure white mist floated among the trees. From the tender grass and sage clumps drowsy birds made small scolding sounds. Freshness was over the land; only the wood lot was blotched and shadowy. Beside Uriah surly Kant U'Ren looked steadily ahead at the awakening village. Although there was yet no sun, a tidal wash of pale, pale pink touched roof tops.

"Be better," said the half-blood, "if one of us goes in alone, first."

Uriah's reply was instantaneous. "And face them alone if there's trouble?"

Where Lee sat his horse beside Zeke, black fear froze his heart. Uriah had doubts about the villagers. If there was reason to doubt their only allies—what hope was there? He looked at his brother. Zeke was rubbing a bristly jaw; the sound was loud. Behind them sat George Dobkins and Pete Amaya. Dobkins was sucking on his bubbling pipe. Amaya was a ragged bronze statue, motionless and impassive. The long-barreled revolver that had splintered Paxton Clement's skull was jammed into his waist-band.

Finally Uriah led out. They followed him at a brisk walk across the open plow ground, and distantly, where people were stirring, they were seen. Men darted among the shacks and stores. By the time they were close a dozen armed men barred their way into Bethel. Beside Lee, Zeke cursed with cold feeling.

"We'll never get away if they start shooting," he said. "Not over all this open ground."

But Uriah rode on as though unaware of the obvious hostility awaiting them at the village's outskirts. He did not change his lead or slacken his pace until he was ten feet from the band of men afoot. Others were hastening up, also with rifles,

94

hair tousled and hastily dressed but all with the same locked expression.

Town Marshal Will Harper—a sheepman himself—spoke first. "Hold it, Gorman, right where you are. What are you doing here?"

"We're after food and fresh horses," Uriah replied in ice-clear tones. "We also need ammunition."

"Not here you don't," the marshal answered back. "You got the whole god-damned country against you for what you done at XIH. You put all our lives in danger . . . ain't a sheepman in Wyoming isn't in danger now. You ruined our last hope for peace."

"Peace," Uriah choked. "Peace with the cowmen? Damn you, Harper. There was never a hope for peace and you know it."

"You been outlawed by the U.S. marshal, Gorman. You and those that ride with you." Will Harper's eyes flicked over them one by one. "The governor's sending troops . . . the cowmen're hiring guns . . . there's posses all over the country looking for you. The folks here in Bethel want no part of you. Now go on . . . ride off."

"Harper, we got to have vittles."

"Get 'em somewhere else. Now go on."

Harper raised his rifle. The men around him did likewise. By now they numbered close to twenty guns. Harper's small eyes glowed spitefully, murderously.

"I already lost a hundred woollies. Them as are riding with you'll lose more. You aren't free-graze men any more, you're a bunch of damned outlaws . . . renegades. You'll have prices on your heads before many more days. Now ride off or we'll bury you right here."

"There'll be a sight more digging than you figure on if you try it," Uriah said harshly. But he drew back on his reins and turned his horse.

They followed him back across the plow ground, each head twisted, watching the silent men back at the village. Near the tag end of the silent file Kant U'Ren growled: "They won't try it. No rewards yet to make it worth the risk."

Uriah rode slumped over. What some thought with sinking hearts was dejection, though, was thoughtfulness. He halted when they were back against the warming hills.

"Pete, take whoever you want and go steal us some horses. Remember, we got to have good sound ones . . . and fast ones, too."

Amaya nodded. His teeth flashed. He chose George Dobkins and Gaspar Pompa.

"Fawcett," Uriah continued, "you take who you want and fetch us back food and as much ammunition as you can get . . . pistol and rifle." Joseph Fawcett watched Uriah impassively; he made no move to do as ordered until Uriah swept the others with his brittle stare.

"The rest of you'll come with me. We'll go to C Bar S."

"What for?" Zeke asked.

"To get Simpson and his boy." The burning eyes swept over them. "Hostages, you fools. We got to have hostages before we can barter with the law or the Army . . . I know."

Joseph Fawcett's eyes flickered with faint hope. He turned and selected three men. Among them was Kant U'Ren.

When they split up, the sun was climbing high. Counting Uriah, the last band to skirt along the hills southwesterly numbered six men. As usual Lee found his place beside Zeke. They moved onward in deep silence.

The sun at its fierce height burned down. In all that throbbing solitude it beat against them, reflected from the mountain sides. They could not escape it; they hugged the rocky upthrusts for protection against sentinel eyes and it engulfed them. Lee grew drowsy. Thirst dried his throat and his face felt raw and red. Beside him Zeke rode without a murmur, granite-like even as Uriah was also granite-like.

Uriah did not speak. He did not have to. They all knew the way to the Simpson Ranch, and after that . . . planning did no good. You acted as you had to when the time came.

"Zeke?" Lee said.

"Yeah."

"Was Harper talking the truth?"

"I reckon. We been outlawed all right . . . I already told you that."

"Then what in hell are we doing here? Why aren't we getting out?"

Zeke's eyes, fixed on Uriah's back, were dull and murky. He shrugged without replying.

"Zeke, we can't fight the Army."

"Maybe we won't have to. The old man's been figuring."

Lee looked ahead where their father rode. Uriah's bony shoulders were rigid. His raw-boned frame was incongruous-looking on the horse, long shanks dangling, ragged shirt half in, half out of his waistband, big pistol at his side and naked-winking rifle balancing across the saddle fork. Lee's darkness of spirit returned. Once again he was divided within himself.

"Zeke?"

"Yeah."

"I been thinking. The way he's been acting lately . . . since that first killing at Shipman's Meadow . . . and all . . ."

"Well?"

"Zeke, I think Paw's crazy."

The younger man's importuning eyes were met by a hard, cold stare. "Boy," the older brother said in a soft and distant way. "He's your paw . . . don't you ever forget that. He gave you life. He's bent-shouldered from raising you and me."

98

The solid wall of Zeke's blind allegiance grew between them. In substance it was nearly tangible. Lee grew silent. They followed their father with faces averted from one another.

Suddenly, growing from stillness, a low, insistent rhythm began to roil the air. It grew louder and Uriah jerked back to a halt, listening. The sound increased, beat up into the steady throb of oncoming horsemen. Uriah looked back at them. His face was sweaty and twisted.

"Up that little draw," he snapped. "Quick now!"

They scattered into the brush of a ravine like quail. Where Uriah dismounted, standing at his horse's head to pinch off any nickering, the others followed his example. Then, a half mile off, where the trail they had been using swung away from the hills to breast the plain, they saw them—a large body of horsemen moving steadily toward them at a loose lope.

"Ander," Uriah breathed. "Looks like he's got half Union City with him."

One of the men behind Lee spoke clearly. "Be a hanging bee if they find us." He crouched closer to his horse with sweat dripping off his chin.

"Keep low and still," Uriah cautioned as the riders swung with the trail and came closer. "If we're caught watch me . . . do as I do."

Lee was sick with dread and fear. Beside him big Zeke looked calm except for the sudden whiteness around dark-ringed eyes.

The riders streamed past, every eye sweeping the long run of land ahead. Their leader, Town Marshal Bob Ander, showed a glimpse of haggard face and bitter eyes, then he was gone and the others were gone after him. Choking dust lingered in their wake. It dulled the sound of Uriah's voice.

"Charley and Dade weren't with them, boys. It's a good sign." He led his horse out of the brush and toed into the stirrup. "They'll be at the ranch. Come on."

Lee followed his father, thinking that Will Harper had been right, terribly right. The land was alive with men bent on their destruction. When Zeke rode close, Lee said: "He's going to get us all killed."

Zeke might not have heard. At least his head didn't turn or his eyes show understanding. He was watching their father's back and rocking along at a gallop.

Overhead an evil sun glittered across the vast sweep of sky. Below there was an emptiness. Ahead, tall and stringy in the saddle, rawhide-tough and inflexible, was Uriah. Beyond him, coming to sight, assuming a dimensional fix upon the prairie, was a set of log and mud wattle ranch buildings: Simpson's C Bar S.

Uriah reined down. Shiny with sweat, his horse wheeled and cavorted under a tight rein. The old man let them cluster up around him. "We got to be careful," he said, never once looking away from the buildings. "We'll go under the cutbank where the creek lies . . . leave the horses there and go on afoot."

They followed him noiselessly, blindly, out of sight under the creek-scoured dirt barranca that ran behind Simpson's barn and along the south side of his sturdy square house. The horses were left tethered and each man had his gun bared.

Where the creekbed heightened with silted gravel Uriah straightened up to look out. The house was less than fifty feet away. Some scrawny chickens were foolishly busy in an untended vegetable garden. They caught movement and cocked bright and silly eyes at Uriah. A door slammed somewhere nearby. Uriah drew down lower, only his raging eyes showed over the crumbly creekbank. The chickens forgot and returned to their scratching. A man appeared abruptly from the rear of the house. He stood looking northward toward the hills, in the direction Ander's posse had ridden. His expression was fiercely etched and cruel. It didn't even change when Uriah's voice came, thinly drawn out, from the creekbed.

"Don't make a single move, Simpson. Not a single move!"

Chapter Seven

Charles Simpson was a flint-like man, as hard as the land. He watched Uriah over the rim of the creekbank and stood silently. On both sides of Uriah other heads appeared, some hatless. Each face was familiar and Charley Simpson studied them singly. He meant to remember each one. It was his nature, Indian-like, never to forgive nor forget.

"Get his gun," said Uriah.

Zeke scrambled out of the arroyo and went stalking forward. A brace of savage eyes locked, then Zeke emptied Simpson's hip holster and stood back. The others were coming now. There was not a word. Scarcely a sound. Uriah was close. They were of a height, the captive and his captor. They were alike in other ways, too—both stood raw-boned and stringy and both wore expressions blasted from a life that had seldom been easy.

"You better do it and get it done with," said the cowman. "Ander'll be along directly."

There was irony in Uriah's stare. He shook his head. "We saw Ander. He was riding north, not south." Without looking away Uriah spoke aside. "Zeke, search the house. Take the guns and ammunition and food. Hurry."

Zeke jerked his head at Lee. The younger son

accompanied him. They entered the house from the rear. Inside, the atmosphere was unreal. There was an ancient dog—stone deaf—lying on a mothy bear-skin rug. His eyes were tightly closed and he made no stir as Zeke stepped over him to enter the parlor.

A drab thin woman looked up at their entrance. Where they stood, backgrounded by the doorway, filling it, beard-stubbled, dirty, and heavy with weapons, she had expected to see her husband.

"Not a sound," Zeke said quickly when her mouth opened. He started ahead toward a closed door beyond. "The food and shells, Lee. I'll get Dade."

Lee exchanged a long stare with the drab woman. There was a bluish tint under her eyes, a waxiness to her face. "It'll be all right," he said. "Now show me where the food is."

"Yes, I'll show you."

He followed her through another doorway into a shadowy pantry and, beyond, to the kitchen. There, she turned fully to face him.

"Are you a Gorman?"

"Yes'm. Is there a sack?"

She got him one and watched him fill it from the shelves. Her eyes never left him. Somewhere deep in the house came men's voices, then the clump of boots.

"What are you going to do?"

"Take Charley and Dade."

"No!"

He turned, saw her look of fright dissolve to be replaced by an expression of horror and anguish.

"No! Please God . . . have mercy, boy. Don't take them. Please don't take Dade."

"We won't hurt them, ma'am," he said sadly. A pain struck behind his eyes; they filled with a wetness.

The woman sobbed in terrible silence. She staggered. "Burn the house . . . shoot the critters. Don't take my baby!"

A voice beyond the house called sharply: "Lee! Come on!"

He started for the door. The woman's swimming eyes followed him dumbly. She made no sound. He turned back. "They'll be back, Missus Simpson."

Outside, the sunlight stung. Zeke was there to take the sack and frown at him. They were alone in the yard.

"What took so long . . . the others've gone back to the horses."

Lee followed Zeke and despite the malevolent sunlight there was coldness in him.

The others were moving off slowly. Charley and Dade, tied to their stirrups with a lariat apiece around their throats, were being led along like sheep-killing dogs.

Their work was done. All but Lee and Zeke had fresh C Bar S horses. The men were silent but pleased-looking as Uriah led them craftily back toward the rendezvous, being careful to stay to the high country where visibility was best.

They had been in camp two hours before Joseph Fawcett came picking his way through the mountains with Kant U'Ren and the other men with him: Percy Bachelor and Harold Baker. Fawcett had been lucky. Each man was burdened with two sacks of provisions. For once Fawcett's ox-like countenance was alight with a sense of accomplishment. While the plunder was being examined, he told Uriah: "We hit their line camps and roundup shacks. It was like going to the store in Bethel."

Uriah was not elated. Pedro Amaya was long overdue. He sent Zeke and Lee to a promontory to watch for dust so long as daylight should last. He set the others to preparing a meal, then he left them all, went to a jagged slope of rock, and sat there, hunched over, and lost in thought.

On the wind-scourged promontory Zeke sank down against the rattling gravel and heaved a deep sigh. Lee went down beside him. Below them, to the curve of the world, lay a silent unmoving waste of total emptiness.

"He shouldn't have sent them out in broad daylight to steal horses," Lee said quietly, with his eyes roaming the distances.

"The difference is," replied his brother in the

same tired way, "you steal 'em at night and nobody sees you . . . but you don't get 'em back into the hills, either." He yawned mightily and rubbed his eyes. "Don't worry . . . Pete's no novice. He's stolen plenty horses in his time. I'll bet on it. Besides, he's got miles of country to maneuver in. I'm not worrying."

"Zeke, what if the law won't trade with Paw?"

"Why then I expect we'll have to run for it."

"No. I meant what'll happen to the Simpsons?"

Zeke's jaw rippled with muscle. He made no immediate answer. "That's up to him," he said finally, biting it off.

Lee fell into a troubled silence. The last shaft of daylight was glimmering in the west before either of them spoke again. Then it was Zeke, and his tone was that same blending of rough gentleness he often used toward his brother.

"You thinking about the girl?"

"Yes."

"Don't worry. She's better off than you are."

"I wish I could see her."

Zeke drew up on one arm, staring far out. "You can't, so forget it. Look, look north there. It's men driving horses."

They scrambled up, unaware until that moment of the fading hope that had been in them both. Clear upon the still Wyoming evening they heard hoof beats. Zeke stood smiling with his craggy jaw slackened in the first real pleasure he'd known in days. Beside him stood Lee, whose smile was less and whose head was strangely canted. His eyes pinched down nearly closed and bead-like in their far staring.

"It's Pete," said Zeke. "I recognize that hat of his."

"Zeke!" Lee's fingers closed down over his brother's arm. "Farther back there . . . way out toward Bethel . . . do you see them?"

The oldest brother went as rigid as a startled hawk. He saw nothing but he heard the alarm in Lee's voice.

"Where? What is it? What d'you see, boy?"

"Big bunch of riders a mile or such behind Pete."

Then Zeke saw them and spun away. "Hurry, the others got to be warned."

They fled down through brush and boulders and burst upon the camp.

"Where's Paw?"

"Here," Uriah said, scenting peril and striding forward into the firelight.

The others sprang up and crowded close. The Simpsons alone did not move but they strained to hear what Zeke was saying.

"Pete's coming from Bethel with horses, Paw, but there's a posse behind him."

Uriah cried an oath. "He wouldn't lead 'em here!"

"We can't take that chance. It looks like Ander's posse," Lee said. "There are a lot of 'em."

"All right," Uriah spoke up quickly. "All right, boys . . . boots and saddles. Make it fast. We'll save Amaya and turn back his bluebelly pursuers. Don't stand there . . . move!"

As the others dashed for their saddles in the gathering dusk, Lee said: "What about the Simpsons?"

Uriah shot a black stare at his prisoners. "Get 'em on horses, boy. Bring 'em along and, if they offer trouble or make an outcry, shoot 'em." He put up a hand, touched his youngest with it briefly, then pushed. "Go on."

In moments they were all astride and following Uriah along faintly seen game trails, twisting and turning and scrambling around side hills toward the prairie beyond. There was no room for passing until the hills sloped outward and broadened where they met flat country. Then Zeke got up where his father was, loped ahead, and drew up, listening. The sound of running horses was close. He twisted in the saddle saying nothing but looking a quick question.

Uriah flagged forward with his arm. "Spread out! Make a line. When the horses come up, stop them. There won't be much time. Get a fresh animal . . . but don't let go your old one until you got the new one saddled." He moved down closer to Zeke, pushed past, and led the way out of the hills.

They scarcely had the cordon established before

the first foam-flecked animals raced up. Someone let off a high cry. They waved their hats and the horses slid to a quivering halt, spewing up dust and stones.

"Now!" Uriah bellowed.

Over the tumult of squealing, snorting horses plunging left and right against their neighbors, the sheepmen moved in. Lee caught a bulging-eyed big gelding the color of wet slate—Grulla-colored. Zeke and Uriah were side-by-side; they ran each other's new mounts together and in the confusion snared them easily. Others were working with equal frenzy. Pete Amaya's shrill scream rose high in the night and Kant U'Ren's cry responded.

Some of the horses escaped and some of the men had to secure aid before catching new mounts, but in the end they came all together in the dust and darkness and Lee retrieved his bound prisoners where he had tied their horses.

"Who is that following you?" Uriah thundered at Amaya.

"Following . . . ?" Pete said swiftly, his eyes widening. "No one is following me . . . I don't think."

Uriah's impatience was showing. "Ride east and spread out." His arm made a slicing movement. "Let them ride between you and the hills . . . then shoot." He whirled away to set the example. The others loped after him.

Lee's Grulla was powerful and excited. He searched the faces moving up and found one. With a sharp call he passed two lead ropes to the man. "Watch 'em," he commanded, and let the Grulla have his head. In moments he was up with Uriah.

"Paw? Don't shoot them here!"

Uriah's voice rolled over the swish of riders. "Boy, it's time you learned to kill good . . . not to live long." He veered away and Lee heard his thundering orders. His voice in the night was drum-like and rumbling; it was without excitement but it held urgency.

Into the quivering sounds came shouts of men and running horses. Lee had only a glimpse of strangers between him and the starkly etched hills, then lancing tongues of flame followed the bursts of gunfire.

Horses screamed and men shouted. There was an interval when no shots came back when the sheepmen poured lead in upon the posse men, downing horses and riders. Then Lee was stunned by the roar of shotguns, nearly blinded by enormous mushrooms of yellow-white gobbets of light. Beside him a man gasped and choked on a gush of blood. He saw him fall and was off his horse in an instant, bending forward. It was the Basque, Gaspar Pompa. He knelt lower and looked into the ashen face, into the liquid dark eyes, soft usually but filled now with an appalling knowledge, reflecting the awful burning behind

Pompa's belt and higher, where buckshot had torn the flesh and shredded the Basque's filling lungs.

There was a roar in Lee's head. He heard no shooting, no screaming, or the slashing of bullets. He saw only the fresh wave of blood running from Pompa's mouth. *He's dying,* he thought. *Gaspar's dying. Oh, Christ, he's dying. . . .*

The Basque's eyes were hotly clear and unmoving. He was holding to consciousness with terrible determination while his lifeblood spilled out, staining the tender grass and the trousers of the big man kneeling beside him. Lee put a hand to Gaspar's face. There was no feeling, no warmth in the tan flesh or in the white flesh. There was only that eternity during which their eyes met and held and shared in that enduring moment the knowledge of hastening death. Then Gaspar Pompa died. Just a puddling of the dark flow of life outward. A gentling of the hot terrible stare. A heavy softening of the broken body against the earth and the Basque was dead.

It was Uriah's searing shout that roused Lee, returned him to awareness and lifted him to his feet.

"Ride! Leave off and follow me!"

He was stooping to catch the loose body in his arms when something struck him, hard, nearly downing him. He flailed for balance and wheeled. It was Zeke, mounted and glaring downward from a contorted face.

111

"Never mind . . . get astride, boy. Hurry!"

"He's dead, Zeke."

"Hubs of hell! You can't help him. . . ." A furious arm, powerful and corded like steel, caught at his shoulder, wrenched him full around, and pushed him fiercely toward his horse.

"Get up, damn you, get up!"

He mounted the plunging Grulla and was borne away with wind whipping against his face. Ahead, dim in the night was the flapping silhouette of his brother and the others, all hastening after Uriah, who was well ahead and who did not turn for a backward look.

They rode hard and, because there was yet no moon, made good their escape. But in fact pursuit would not have come anyway. The Union City posse had lost four dead and seven injured. But the sheepmen did not know this, and even Uriah, who would have been bitterly pleased, forged ahead with green eyes wildly burning and dark with pure fury. In his raging heart he blamed Pete Amaya for leading the posse men to their hide-out. It would no longer be possible to stay in the hills. After tonight the mountains would be swarming with the swelling ranks of their enemies.

He led them far east of Union City and in this his craftiness was evident. The cowmen would be looking for them in the hills, at their lambing grounds perhaps or maybe even at their old camps.

But they would be far across the cowmen's own brush- and boulder-strewn domain, behind the cowmen's town, past most of their ranches even.

Uriah knew of a place where Cottonwood Creek turned marshy and ran sluggishly, where the rise of land stemmed its twisting course and diverted the flow through a tree-girted swampland. He led them there and waited in the humid darkness, prey to thousands of mosquitoes, for the last man to ride up and swing down.

"Joseph!" he called as Fawcett loomed close. "Who did we lose?"

"Dunno," came the hoarse reply.

It was Lee who said: "Gaspar Pompa. They killed him with buckshot."

"Anyone else hit or hurt?" Uriah queried with no sound of compassion or sense of loss in his urgent voice.

"No one else," a voice replied from the tangle of thicket and rip-gut grass underfoot. It was Zeke. He was examining his horse minutely for signs of injury. He found none.

"Amaya!"

"Yes, *jefe*?"

"Didn't you know they were following you!"

"No. I did not know. It was growing dark. The horses made a lot of noise. We watched after we left Bethel. We saw no one, *jefe*. I don't know where they came from. It was good you were close by because our horses were giving out. . . ."

"It wasn't his fault," a wide-shouldered short man said suddenly.

"Who's that?" Uriah demanded.

"Me. Percy Bachelor, and I'm pulling out, Gorman. We could've all got killed tonight. We already lost our sheep, our wagons . . . the only thing left to lose is our god-damned lives and I'm telling you I don't aim to lose mine . . . not just because you got a hankering to win at least one fight in your life."

"Percy . . . ," a threatening voice said in the darkness.

But Uriah interrupted. "Let him go. Let anyone go who wants to. There's no place with me for cowards."

"Cowards!" Percy Bachelor burst out. "Cowards! God damn you, Gorman, I've done every bit as much fighting in my time as you have. But not as an outlaw. What you're doing here is crazy. You got us all broke and hungry and outlawed with your killing. What's ahead? More killing, more hunger and running until every man jack is dead. Hung dead or shot dead . . . but dead."

Zeke was crashing toward the mounted man through swamp creepers and rip gut. "Get out!" he roared at Bachelor. "Ride out and keep on going. And if you ever mention us to anyone and I'm able . . . I'll hunt you down. Now get!"

Bachelor left, riding his foam-flecked horse

south, the only way that was safe and open. The others moved without speaking, their boot steps snapping twigs and making sucking sounds in the swamp mud. The only man among them who found bitter pleasure in this dissension was bound Charley Simpson. Now he said: "The rest of you listen. What that man told you is right. Gorman's going to get you all killed."

Uriah was beside his prisoner in five big strides. He struck the bound man down and stood over him with murder in his face. Dade Simpson struggled upright but he was caught from behind and held.

"Do that again," said Uriah to the fallen cowman, "and I'll kill you with my bare hands . . . alone."

"Sure you will," Simpson swore right back. "As long as you got me tied, you will."

"Untie him!" Uriah roared.

But Lee was there to counsel another course and eventually Uriah stalked away. Lee helped Simpson to his feet; he wiped with a dirt-encrusted sleeve at the trickle of blood at the cowman's mouth.

"Don't push him," he told Simpson. "Leave him be."

Charles Simpson turned his hot stare to the younger man's white face, blurred by shadows. He did not speak.

There was nothing to eat so they hobbled the

horses, made up pallets on dry ground, and sank down in total silence with the heat of battle dead in them. Only Uriah still moved; he paced through the blackness of night following the bent of his thoughts and thinking swiftly. It was not in him ever to be defeated, and yet in his lifetime he had never triumphed.

He stalked now beyond the hungry bivouac, remembering other dark and cheerless nights; nights like this one when the unfinished matrix of his life was starkly in mind, soaringly unpleasant and goading. He was outlawed. They were all outlawed. Ahead lay more fleeing, more fighting, more burning lancets of flame in the dark. And yet it was in the cause of right he did these things; it was the law that was wrong. The law and the priority of men who thought because they had come first into Wyoming that they owned it, owned the free-graze that was Public Domain.

Was it inevitable that he use his years fighting for causes lost? *If need be,* he thought. *If need be.* It was not his right to question—only to obey the dictates of a strong heart and a resolute mind. The world was not a good place; it was full of wrong. Even when a man sought with his arms to coax a living from it, without trouble, he could not do it.

There in the mud beside the far Missouri he had kneeled in squalor and want and put down his wife. There at Appomattox he had sat in numb want. Here in Wyoming he had wrestled with the land and a few head of woollies to do no more than keep his gut full. And as in those other places there was that which would deny him, which would take away his right to stand upright and vie with others for a free way of life made by choice.

He came upon a rotten stump soggy with moss and lichen. He sat upon it.

But, Lord, he was tired. A man's spirit wearies. It was more than a sagging of the flesh. It was the knowledge, first held at middle-age or beyond, that what the future holds is not happiness or pleasure or even surcease. It is struggle and deprivation and want, until death comes. It was the God-given sight to see ahead and those who had it knew inevitable tiredness because the future was only bright and promising so long as you could not see into it. He *could* see; he had seen. That was why he had not railed at Percy Bachelor. Because he knew in his heart Bachelor had been right.

There was no way out. There was never a compromise with death. You went to meet it a little each day. You could not change that.

He looked through the sap-filling tree limbs to a fully black heaven. He had the sight now. He knew his future as thoroughly as he knew anything. It was as Bachelor had said. Well, if there was gall in the knowledge, there was also comfort in that certainty. He would plan it so that the free-graze war would be his greatest battle.

He took his secret and his stiffening body back to the core of the camp and sank down there. All but one of the others were dead asleep. Lee, his youngest, was dark-limned against the fullness of night, awake, but turned away from Uriah. Lee was thinking, too, but differently, and of other things. Pompa's stark stare full with the knowledge of death. His out-flared nostrils and the senseless scrabbling of his fingers in the moistening earth. In other days his laughter, his flashing teeth, and his huge smiles, half wry, half apologetic when they had poked fun at his English. Ann carrying the burden of their sin hard under her heart now. Carrying also the stigma of their love and facing those of her kind, and other kinds, who stared with steel-bright eyes because she was quickening to life another soul—from the loins of a sheepman.

With his insides shrinking Lee thought of these things. Nearby, Charley and Dade Simpson, watching him through slitted lids, gave it up. He was the only one remaining awake. He would not sleep this night. There was no chance of escape. The Simpsons lay back and relaxed and slept. Of them all only Lee could not sleep.

Chapter Eight

In the morning Uriah told them that Harold Baker had deserted in the night and that they could no longer stay where they were lest Baker betray them in exchange for clemency.

Lee looked at his brother. Zeke did not meet his gaze but started for the horses with the others. No one said anything until they were mounted, then George Dobkins said: "We got to get something to eat pretty quick. Besides, I'm plumb out of tobacco."

Uriah listened with his back to the others, then he nodded. Beyond the trees where he was staring was raw country, throbbing with summer's heat rising higher with each passing hour.

When Uriah gathered his reins, Joseph Fawcett spoke up hoarsely: "You're not going out there, are you? Why, hell, Uriah, they can see us for miles."

"Baker made the choice, I didn't." Uriah turned his horse and stared at them.

Lee was shocked at the change in him. Even Zeke was astonished and sat rigidly in his saddle on the far side of the hostages.

"You hear me well and remember what I tell you. They made the rule of fang and law apply, we didn't. So far we've more than carried our side of it. There's more'n luck protecting us . . . you remember that. Now come on."

They followed him dutifully but sluggishly. There were eleven of them, excluding the Simpsons. They rode in single file strung out like Indians. Lee's prisoners seemed sunken in lethargy. Dade's lips were shriveled and cracked. Lee held the canteen for him to drink. Charles Simpson watched this, and kept his eyes on the youngest Gorman for some time afterward.

Uriah led them in an arcing ride to the north-west, around Union City. They came upon a narrow run of water, a tributary of Cottonwood Creek. It was shallow, fetlock-deep. They crossed it, then dismounted on the far side and drank, watered their animals and refilled canteens. There was no shade along the stream but there was coolness. They were disposed to rest a moment, to savor this relief as long as they might. But Uriah ordered them astride and led them onward. Again they obeyed in dumb silence.

He was heading for the hills again, but northerly, far from their sheep camps. Once they spied a yellow dust banner rising over swift-moving horsemen and paused to watch. The posse made a wide swing and turned southward toward Union City.

Lee's breath ran out fully. "They didn't see us," he told Zeke. There was no reply.

Where the prairie dipped, then lifted, rising toward splotchy foothills, Pete Amaya trilled a warning and pointed back with an upflung arm. "Soldiers!" he called out.

There was no mistaking the measured cadence or disciplined distances kept by this second band of horsemen. They were troopers all right, and they, too, were heading for Union City. Uriah's face was a dust-streaked mask. He watched in hard silence, the look in his strange eyes hidden behind pouches of flesh.

Trees appeared on the slopes. They rode through meager shade, and soon they came to a clearing that rose slowly to a good height, their horses' legs swishing through wiry grass. Uriah dismounted and bent to hobble his horse. The others followed his example wordlessly as they had come to do. Only the Simpsons stood rooted, waiting. When Uriah arose to slip his mount's bridle off and hang it on the saddle horn, the elder Simpson spoke.

"You goin' to starve us to death, Gorman?"

"It would be quicker to kill you."

Uriah's answer brought several heads around. Dull eyes looked, not with speculation or even interest, but with full knowledge that Uriah might draw his gun. They wanted only to be clear of flying bullets.

But Uriah stared down Charley Simpson. The prisoner sank upon the ground and slumped, eyes closed and lips loosely hanging, a picture of defeat.

"Zeke, take Joseph and go get us something to eat."

The elder son took wiry Pete Amaya, whose natural diffidence was entirely gone now. He rode like an Indian and looked like one in filthy, ragged clothing, only his weapons bright and shiny. Lee watched them pick a route along the foothills westerly, screened by trees and bracken. Uriah's sudden voice snagged his attention. Uriah was standing tall with his back to the bony mountains, looking down where they sprawled in the hot dust.

"We'll wait until they fetch back food. Then we'll go to Union City."

Each body stiffened. Every head drew up erect. Joseph Fawcett's sagging jaw snapped closed— then open again. "Union City . . . ?"

"We'll be safe. We've got hostages." Uriah scanned them singly. His face gaunt with thinness, his time-tempered whiskers grayer with dust and frayed-looking. And his eyes nearly closed in a long squint. "We're going to offer them peace in exchange for freedom of movement for our sheep, and equal rights on the range."

Kant U'Ren was staring at Uriah. There was a new expression on his face, a look of wonder, of doubt, of a growing certainty about something nebulous. When Uriah became silent, he spoke into the hush. "We'll get bullets. They won't bargain. Uriah, we're murderers. We're outlaws. You take us down . . . there won't a one of us come back."

"Murderers?" Uriah challenged in a swift-rising voice. "Who killed the first man? Not us."

"Don't change nothing," the half-breed argued. "They control the law. They got soldiers on their side. What we did at XIH'll hang every man jack of us if we go down there. You ought to know that." U'Ren returned Uriah's fierce stare with unwavering courage. "I told you to kill them kids and the old woman. I told you . . . but no. Now they got witnesses against us."

"Their witnesses did not see Paxton die."

U'Ren sighed and wagged his head. "That's book law maybe," he answered. "It ain't range law. If they get their hands on us, we won't get near a law court."

There was a murmur of agreement among the others. Uriah's face flamed with wrath, his lips drew out stonily, and his fists were clenched. He glared at the half-blood.

"Maybe you'd like to leave, too. Maybe you'd like to find Bachelor and Baker and make a run for it."

"No," U'Ren said without heat. "It's too late for that. Bachelor might make it . . . he left in the night. Baker sure as hell won't."

Silence descended over the little camp. Lee slept for an hour, then awakened. Around him others were lying out flat, while some snored. Charley Simpson was craning his neck southward where a spiral of dust moved from west to east, hope was in his face with painful clarity. Lee looked away from it, looked straight up at the brassy blue sky where a lowering sun rode golden-yellow and immense. Around him was a full throbbing solitude. The sun at its great height burned down. The ground was hard against his flesh. His thoughts were quiet things, very rational and orderly and torturous. If Uriah got his kind of peace with the cowmen—which would never come to pass—the cowmen would let the Simpsons die many times over before they would agree to equal rights for sheepmen. But if Uriah got his peace as he wanted it—there would be more blood spilled, more fights. It had always been that way. Wherever Uriah had led them, there had been antagonism and unpleasantness.

It hadn't always been Uriah's fault, true, but it had been like that, nevertheless, and he didn't want to spend his years and his strength fighting. He wanted to live, to grow things, to marry and have young. . . .

Ann.

He closed his eyes and went back the trail into memory. It was so vivid, so clear to relive in his mind. But only for moments. You couldn't continually relive something like that and not destroy it. It was a memory to be cherished, to be hoarded, and relived rarely. It was a kind of wealth you could squander into meaninglessness by constant reference. He would not do that, because it might be the only beautiful memory he would have. He would not destroy it.

Leave, his mind said suddenly. *Get up and ride off . . . leave while you still can.*

He could go back secretly to the Fosters. He could lie hidden until Ann came out. She would go with him and they could escape. He knew they could.

The apathy fell away. His body tensed against the ground. A desperate sense of urgency swept over him. He raised up and looked around. They were asleep. All but the Simpsons and Uriah, who had gone off somewhere to be alone. They were sprawled in exhaustion and dullness. His hand slithered over the ground, his body was seized with trembling, a great burden lifted off his spirit. He half started to his feet, and then he saw Zeke and Pete Amaya returning through the shadows of dying day and his brother's face was gray and bloodless with a weariness that went deeper than bone and muscle, and while he looked into his brother's face, the headiness dissipated, and in that moment he knew he was lost. He could not do it. He could not desert them like this.

He sank back down with pain moving behind his eyes, with shame and terrible sadness in him. He had no clear thought. He only knew he could not leave them.

Zeke was calling. Ahead of him, already dismounted from his head-hung horse, Pete

Amaya was emptying a jute sack and grinning from ear to ear. The others were coming to life, blinking and sitting up and exhaling foul breath. Uriah came out of the underbrush, too, and Lee saw the look of approval on his face, then he got up with the others and stumbled forward, almost blindly. Lee could not leave them in treachery.

Zeke stood back, watching the others tear at the food. He and Pete had already eaten, he told them, but he would drink coffee. As they made the little dry-oak fire that gave off no smoke, Zeke turned his horse out and sprawled near them, long legs thrust out fully, aching body going soft against the ground. Uriah asked about the food, and Zeke told him. His words carried no threat at first, while the others ate, but later they did.

"There's a big posse camped between us and the camps," he said. "We saw them from the hills. When they rode off, we raided their cache."

"How big a posse?" Uriah asked, around a mouthful.

"Maybe thirty of 'em. I recognized old Matt Karnahan from over by Chugwater. The others were strangers."

Uriah repeated the name thoughtfully. "Chug-water. That means they're recruiting outsiders." His grinding jaws grew still. "Which way did they ride, boy?"

"Toward the camps . . . back into the hills where we left the woollies."

The men went on eating but Uriah heeded. "They'll scatter the bands . . . probably drive them off some bluff."

"Yes, I think so."

"They can't find us so they'll take it out on our sheep."

Lee went to his brother with a tin mug of coffee. "You better sleep, Zeke. We're riding out tonight."

The eldest son reached for the cup and sipped from it. "Riding out where?"

"To Union City with our hostages."

"What?"

"That's what Paw says."

Zeke finished the coffee without looking again at his brother. He put the cup aside and faced toward their father. A throbbing vein swelled at his temple but his voice did not change.

"Paw?"

"Yes, boy?"

"You're not taking anyone to Union City tonight."

Uriah sensed the rising rebellion. But more than that he felt growing anger and surprise. Zeke had never, in all his years, contradicted him before. He pushed away the food and turned where he hunkered. He checked the anger and said quietly: "They won't dare do anything while we have hostages. We'll give them our terms. They'll accept and the free-graze war'll be finished. It's got to be that way, Zeke."

127

"They're thicker'n grass down there, Paw. And there are soldiers. They'll let you kill the Simpsons . . . then they'll kill you."

"No," Uriah replied, still in that foreign way of speaking, quiet and gentle. "No, son, we'll go by stealth. You know there never was a cowman could match us in that. We'll get Bob Ander and one or two others of them and we'll make our peace."

There was something coming here, the others knew. They rolled their eyes and twisted to watch and listen. Zeke had never in all their recollections challenged Uriah before.

"Paw, Pete and me saw at least thirty armed men in one posse this afternoon. There's at least two more posses out just as big. There are soldiers . . . maybe a hundred of them. You saw them. We all saw them. Listen to me a minute."

Uriah got suddenly to his feet and stood rigid. The bloodless line of his lips was razor-thin; his beard reflected the oak firelight, dull red, and his tawny unkempt white thatch stood askew. To Catholic-raised Pedro Amaya, looking in awe, he was Moses on the Mount. To the others he was towering wrath personified. They shrank from looking at him. Only Kant U'Ren peered inside his shirt for an insect that had bitten him, and ignored both Uriah and his eldest son.

"Paw, I don't know who's right and who's wrong. All I know is that what little we had is gone now. Maybe if we'd just hide out a spell, things would die down. Then we could gather what's left of the bands and go away. Down to Colorado or over into Idaho. Start over again clean."

Uriah was still standing, stockstill and silent, sharp-pointed shoulders stark against the gathering night, burning eyes unblinking on the face of his eldest son.

"We lost Manuel Cardoza, Gaspar Pompa, and the others. They've lost old Clement, Slocum, Hoag, and Hogan. Paw, let's not lose everything."

Uriah's voice came finally, echoing like distant thunder. "Answer me, boy! Would you rather live on your knees or die on your feet?"

Zeke's gray face tightened perceptibly. Throughout the camp there was stillness. He made no immediate reply but got stiffly to his feet. They were equally as tall, as big-boned and craggy, but Zeke was thirty pounds heavier, and now he returned the old man's stare doggedly.

"I'd rather live on my feet," he answered. "It can come out that way if you'll let it."

The exploding fury of Uriah's glare was strong with near-madness. Zeke braced into it, but Lee, standing beside him, flinched as though from a blow.

"You!" Uriah ground out in bitter scorn. "Of all people . . . *you!* Turning on me. Father in heaven, I never thought I'd live to see this day!"

"Paw, listen to me . . ."

"No! You're a coward, Zeke. You're like your brother . . . you got your maw's blood in you. All the Hairstons was cowards."

"Listen to me! There's something else in the back of your head. I got no way of knowing what it is, but it's there, Paw. You want to lead a band of guerrillas against the cowmen and the soldiers . . . you want to hit 'em hard and fade away before 'em. You think they'll make peace out of fear, but they won't. Everyone here knows they won't. Please, Paw . . . not Union City."

Uriah said no more. He turned his back fully upon his sons and glared at the others. They hid their eyes from him, sat rooted and hushed, and then he whirled and went storming out into the thickening darkness. They heard the crashing of his progress through underbrush and sat awkwardly still, their hunger gone.

Lee went over to the fire and poked at it. No one looked at him. Only Kant U'Ren moved. He refilled a cup with coffee and leaned back to sip it. His black stare was broodingly fixed on the thin flames that sparkled under Lee's stick. Zeke dropped down again, back against his saddle. He picked up some small stones and filtered them through nerveless fingers. George Dobkins asked someone for tobacco. Moments later his pipe was bubbling syrupy and a strong fragrance rose.

Joseph Fawcett got up eventually and stalked

beyond the perimeter of faint red light. He paused once and turned back. "Lee? Come here a minute, will you?"

Lee went, followed Fawcett far out where the trees were thicker and the land began a slow outfall toward the prairie, south. There, he squatted when the older man did likewise. Joseph Fawcett was uneasy. He had to force the words out.

"Lee, I got to say this. Your brother's right. Listen . . . the countryside's swarming with them. We'll be hard put just to stay alive. If he leads us to Union City, we'll all get killed. I don't mean no disrespect to your daddy, boy . . . you know I rode with him to XIH and I've done everything he's asked of me. But this . . . this riding to certain death . . . is no good." Fawcett's dull eyes lifted briefly to Lee's face, then dropped swiftly away. "I'm leaving. I got to, Lee. But first I wanted the others to understand I'm not sneaking out like Harold Baker did. And I'm not going up against Uriah like Percy Bachelor, either. I'm just going . . . is all. . . . You understand, Lee?"

The swiftly falling Wyoming night was down fully now. There was a black-breathing stillness that lasted until the first crickets came out to chirp. Overhead, a scimitar moon rode serenely through a purple, curving vault. Lee's face was pale. He was choking and for a time he could not speak. *I'll go with you, Fawcett. I'll get my horse*

131

and ride with you. We'll go by the Fosters' place and get Ann, then we'll ride by night and hide by day until we're far south in Colorado.

He stood up.

Joseph Fawcett got to his feet, also.

They looked long at one another before the older man half turned away with his face averted.

"I got no bright ideals like your paw has, boy. I never been smart enough for things like that. I know sheep and I don't mind herding them in the hills. I like the hills . . . they're sort of protective . . . they sort of fold around a man and cradle him. You know?"

Lee spoke swiftly, finally. He had to speak that way for the words to be steady. "Go on, Fawcett. I won't say anything until Paw asks. That'll give you a fair start."

"Tell Zeke good bye for me. . . . Take care, Lee."

"Good bye."

Chapter Nine

Uriah did not reappear until 10:00 p.m. He noticed at once the absence of Joseph Fawcett, but, before he spoke of it, he went out where the horses stood drowsing, gutted-up on grass, and gassy. Then he stormed back to the quiet ring of men around the dead fire.

"Where's Fawcett?" he demanded. "His horse is gone."

"Gone," Kant U'Ren answered, at the same time jerking his head sideways at Lee. "Ask him."

"Lee . . . ?"

"He's gone, Paw. He said Zeke was right. He said he thought you'd get us all killed."

Uriah choked on his wrath. "The sniveling coward," he ground out in bitterness and scorn. "The yellow-bellied scum!"

From farther back in the darkness Zeke said: "He rode with us to XIH. He went foraging and he never hung back about anything."

Uriah seemed to grow taller, drawing himself up. He stood a long moment in total silence, then spun away toward the horses. "Come on. We're still ten strong."

The others got to their feet in blind obedience. One of the last to arise was Lee. He did not move out with the others right away but watched his brother heading Uriah off just short of their mounts.

Zeke's hand was on his father's arm. "Paw . . . don't. You'll make it worse."

"Take your hand off me!"

"Then quit this craziness, Paw."

Uriah's free arm swung swiftly. Twice the bony fist cracked against Zeke's jaw. Then Uriah wrenched free. "You damned whelp!" he bellowed. "You ungrateful coward!"

With a fearful roar that drowned Uriah's words, Zeke lunged. The old man sprang back, as much

133

in surprise as in defense. He recovered swiftly and a scraggly fist swirled up and out, crashing squarely into Zeke's unprotected face. It would have downed a lesser man; it only jarred Zeke and it did not stop his rush. Then Uriah side-stepped like a cat, his face gone livid, and fired his other fist. Zeke saw this one coming and went in under it, big arms reaching, fingers crooked. There was a flung-back trickle of blood along one cheek from the torn corner of his mouth.

No one spoke; no one scarcely breathed. It had happened too suddenly, this abrupt bursting into flames of a smoldering antagonism. Lee rushed forward, but George Dobkins stopped him with an upflung arm as hard as iron.

"No, boy," Dobkins said with swift urgency. "Let 'em get the poison out. Leave 'em be."

Lee subsided, stood rock-like with the others, watching.

Uriah's neck was scarlet. His face was darkened by the blood that roared in his head now, as it had roared through fifty years of fighting. He was long of tooth at this game and back-stepped away from Zeke's rush at the same time throwing looping blows that Zeke made no attempt to avoid. It was as though the elder son wanted to be struck, wanted to absorb all that Uriah could punish him with as he bored in.

Then Uriah tripped over a flung down saddle and fell. Zeke bent low, feeling for him. Uriah scrambled frantically to free himself of the leather, but Zeke's hooked fingers found him, closed like iron around his legs and yanked him free, pulled him flat on his back through the rising black dust.

Uriah twisted and wrenched and tore this way and that, seeking to break free. He knew what was coming and fought, panther-like, to avoid it. Then Zeke's hands went up along the writhing body, lifted his father bodily, braced against the frantic scrabbling, and locked behind Uriah's back. Zeke lowered his head, pushed it hard into Uriah's body to save his eyes from clawing fingers. Then he began to squeeze slowly, inexorably, crushed inward until his muscles leaped and quivered snake-like while Uriah's breath whistled out and a rain of futile blows landed upon Zeke's head. He continued to crush until his father's eyes bulged and his mouth sprang open, all pink and wet with snags of discolored teeth showing. Uriah's lips turned blue and his cheeks mottled, but his flailing fists scarcely slackened although their power to hurt was gone.

Then Kant U'Ren stepped up behind Zeke and brought his pistol barrel overhand against the eldest son's skull. It was the only sound.

Zeke collapsed, his arms fell away, and Uriah lay writhing upon the ground, still conscious but only dimly so. Then U'Ren faced around toward

Lee. It was the only quarter from which he expected trouble.

George Dobkins and Pete Amaya went to Uriah and supported him in a sitting position. Another man brought a tin cup of water.

Lee kneeled beside his brother, who was moaning. U'Ren had not struck hard, only hard enough. "Water," the youngest son said. Another man came forward with a cup.

When Uriah could focus his eyes, he looked over where his sons were. "I'll kill him," he cried huskily. "By God, I'll kill him."

Kant U'Ren stepped forward, put a hand under Uriah's arm, and lifted. "No need for that," he said. "Just leave him here. The cowmen'll do it for you. Ain't no sheepman going to live more'n a day or two now, by himself."

"His own father," Uriah gasped, his head full of dizziness and his rib cage burning with pain. "To his own flesh and blood . . ." He blinked wetly. There were winking specks of color before his eyes. He let off a long rattling breath and shook free of supporting arms. "Now come on. We've got a long way to go."

Lee was left alone with his brother.

Zeke stirred, opened wide his eyes, and looked hazily upward through pools of pain. "You . . . ?" he said to Lee.

"No, it wasn't me. It doesn't matter who did it, anyway. Here . . . drink this water."

Zeke drank. Then he explored the sticky welt at the back of his head and Lee got him unsteadily to his feet.

"We don't have any whiskey, Zeke."

His brother's voice got strong quick. "It doesn't matter, boy." He started forward toward the dead fire. George Dobkins materialized suddenly, leading three horses. Zeke blinked at him and waited, saying nothing.

"You coming, Zeke?" Dobkins asked, pushing forward the reins to Zeke's saddled horse.

"What do you care whether I come or not?" Zeke demanded, studying the older man's face.

Dobkins's reply was both toneless and practical. "Ten guns are better'n eight, Zeke. We'll need you . . . both of you." He pushed the reins into Zeke's hand.

"Was it you hit me, George?"

"No, it wasn't me," Dobkins answered. Then, thinking as Lee had thought, also, he added: "It don't matter who it was, Zeke. Come on . . . they won't wait for us."

Lee got his horse from Dobkins. They mounted and shuffled out where the others were getting astride. Many level glances were turned toward them but not a single face showed anything. Each man was thinking his own thoughts and hiding them behind impassivity and silence.

Uriah led them, stiff in the saddle and pain-racked but unwilling for others to see him like

137

that. Behind him rode Kant U'Ren. The others trailed after, single file and soundless. The last two riders were Zeke and Lee Gorman.

Lee could tell from his brother's expression that Zeke regretted what he had done, and he understood that. Not too long before he himself had considered rebelling, but in a less open manner. Remembering made shame redden his face. But there was consolation in knowing that loyal Zeke, more like the old man than anyone else, had also set himself against what they were now riding to do.

As they rode Lee closed his eyes, squeezed them tightly shut, and bobbed along in time with his Grulla mount. There were whispering voices within him. It was hard to disassociate them from the muttered huskings of Pete Amaya and the shapeless silhouette swaying along just ahead of the Mexican. Only by opening his eyes could Lee disseminate the voices.

"I never met a man like the *jefe* before," Amaya was saying. "He is like iron . . . like an Apache. He does not change his purpose."

"I hope I never meet another like him," the other man said softly, thinking he would not be heard.

"He is like a fox."

"More like a wolf, Pete."

"Yes, more like a wolf."

"A rabid one. You know he'll get us all shot or hung, don't you?"

"No, I don't know that," the Mexican retorted. Then added: "It is the risk we take." Thin shoulders rose fatalistically and fell. "We have no better leader . . . besides, it is as he says . . . one does better to die on one's feet than live on one's knees."

The swaying shape twisted. For a moment a white face showed, then the rider straightened around and fell silent. Lee and Zeke saw this, and they were both confident that Amaya missed the purpose of that brief, incredulous stare. Zeke reined closer to his brother, his voice dropped.

"He's always been right. Ever since I can remember Paw's always been right."

"Now you don't think he is."

"It's more'n that, Lee. It's something else as well, boy. He's changed. Since we went to XIH . . . maybe even before that, I don't know, but he's changed since this thing has started."

"Zeke, I would have run away with Ann that time."

Zeke wagged his head softly. "No, you wouldn't have, Lee. Now you would . . . but not then you wouldn't have. Now you won't get the chance, but that's all right. I guess a man's got to come to know something some time or another. I guess if I'd fully believed in what I was doing tonight I'd have killed him."

"You didn't believe what you said to him?"

"I believed it. I still believe it. Going to Union

City's the craziest thing he's ever done. But that's not it. It's blood being thicker'n water, Lee. I guess with me it's always been even thicker'n with you. I can't remember when I haven't been getting between you and Maw and Paw. I'm like him, that's why, only I haven't lived his life so I can still see things different." Zeke straightened up in his saddle. "Look at him sitting up there like Lord Almighty. That's what he's been to us all our lives, Lee. Me even more'n you. That's why I'm riding along behind him when I know a cussed sight better." Zeke's green eyes, so like Uriah's eyes, turned fully on Lee. "That's why you're riding after him . . . you and these other damned fools. He's a sort of symbol to you." Zeke's chapped lips drew downward. "We aren't the first idiots to follow a crazy man into the grave and I reckon we won't be the last."

His brother's words had a profound effect upon Lee. It was their grim sound of certain defeat more than their meaning that pierced him through and left him shaken. He could fight, yes, but he didn't want to fight. He didn't want to die. He wanted to live and grow things, to watch sunlight fade in the west, to feel Ann's sweat-hot flesh against his flesh. And what Zeke had said back at the knoll had been starkly true. The old man was doing this crazy thing because of some reason other than bargaining with their enemies. He had some secret purpose in mind. Something within him had to be satisfied with bravado and it probably would get some of them killed.

It wasn't simply equal range rights that motivated him. He didn't have that much feeling for anything. He just plain didn't. He'd grubbed in Tennessee and Alabama and Missouri. He'd turned his back on each of those places without a second glance or thought, and all the while this strangeness had been growing in his head until now, still lacking the feeling that should have been driving him to wage war for equality and survival, he was fighting instead for this secret thing, even though the men who followed him did not know it yet—all that is, except the sons who knew him this well.

"What is it, Zeke?"

Lee's older brother turned back from gazing far out where an abandoned ranch lay soft-lit in their passing. "What is what? That old ranch? I'd say it's a place that folks left until the trouble's over."

"No, not that."

"What then?"

"Oh, I guess nothing." Lee turned his pale face away.

The night continued darkly still. Beyond the sound of their passing there was only hushed silence. Uriah led them steadily ahead. He told them nothing, hadn't spoken to any of them since he'd left the gravelly knoll far back. Out ahead like he was, none could see the tears that blurred his vision, the bitter working of his mouth from which fell no audible sound. He led them and they followed, and when a sprinkling of golden lamp glow showed far ahead winking down the miles, he swung south and westward and no one questioned his lead, although several of them looked perplexed. Zeke and Lee exchanged a puzzled look. He was not, as they had anticipated, going to lead them directly into Union City, but was instead making a circuitous reconnaissance. He was crafty they knew, and from this they took heart. They might survive after all.

Then Uriah halted them below the town with a rigid arm and drew off alone to fade into the watery light cast by a thin moon. He didn't return for a quarter of an hour and meanwhile they talked in hushed tones among themselves.

Charley Simpson craned his neck toward Lee and Zeke. His face was wire tight and shadowed beneath his hat. "Listen to me," he said sharply. "Don't let him lead you in there."

Kant U'Ren growled: "Shut up, Simpson."

The cowman ignored it. "They won't bargain with you, men. They'll kill the lot of you and us with you."

U'Ren's voice grew stronger. "That'll be too bad for you, won't it?"

Simpson's desperation made him speak louder. "Boys, believe me. I know what I'm talking about. They won't agree to his terms."

"I said shut up!" U'Ren's arm rose and fell, a quirt's knobby thongs whistled through the air and thudded viciously against unprotected flesh. Charley Simpson was silent, only a groan got past his locked teeth.

"You son-of-a-bitch," Dade said brokenly.

U'Ren laughed. It was an explosive sound, harsh and scratchy. His arm went up lazily.

Lee could see the heavy quirt poised for descent. "Don't," he called quickly. "Leave him be, Kant."

The half-breed looked back without checking his arm. Zeke seconded his brother. "You heard him, U'Ren. Leave 'em be."

That time the big half-breed heeded. His arm came down slowly. He looked away from the brothers out into the darkness. He was listening. They all heard it. An oncoming horse. It was Uriah. When he came among them he was smiling. He scarcely checked his mount before he motioned them to follow, and turned back. They went slowly, at a soft walk, and distantly a dog barked.

There were other sounds in the town, even music. They heeded them not as Uriah led them past the tar-paper shacks at Union City's southern-most extremity and on around to the east, where residences stood. Where he angled inwardly toward the rear of Main Street's saloons and offices, with houses on each side and flanking them, Lee's forehead grew crumpled with lines.

His brows lowered and smoothed out in a puzzled straight line.

He thought it dangerous and foolish to take them all beyond the twin rows of houses so that, in retreat, they could be raked by hot fire on both sides. He thought, too, of pushing up and correcting Uriah's course. But in the end he shrank back and followed along. Even if Uriah didn't scorn him with his sunken eyes, he'd have an answer. You couldn't speak against him because he had a way of saying things with harsh zeal and soon you doubted if you'd ever been right. Or his towering silences . . .

George Dobkins's strong whisper came urgently beside Lee. "What the hell's he doing up here?"

"I don't know, George."

"Well, shucks, Lee . . . we're boxed in like this."

"Be still and watch him."

They were past the houses now. Ahead lay the littered lots and darkened rear entrances to Main Street's buildings. Then Uriah drew up. He sat like stone for a moment, looking and listening. There was no one abroad on the back streets. Out on Main Street there was noise, but it was neither loud nor quantitatively strong. The hour was late—nearly midnight. That much of Uriah's figuring was flawless. He swung down and held up his reins to Pete Amaya.

"Zeke, Lee, George, you come with me and fetch along the prisoners. The rest of you stay here and watch. If there's trouble, fire one shot."

He turned his back on them, waiting. The loudest sound was of squeaking leather, of dismounting men grunting down and moving softly up beside him. Without looking back again, he started forward with that thrusting, urgent stride of his. They followed.

It was coal-dark behind the stores and saloons. He led them carefully, as though he had been here before recently, which he had, led them straight to a narrow opening between two buildings—called a dogtrot—and up into it as far as the plank walk beyond. At the opening he paused to look north and south, then he stepped out and the others pushed up close around him. There was only a sleeping soldier visible the full length of the roadway. Beyond the soldier in front of a saloon, where listless slow music sounded, was a hitch rack holding less than a dozen sleeping horses, the saddled property of late drinkers.

"Go up and take care of that soldier," Uriah said to his eldest, and, as Zeke slipped forward, he faced the others, green eyes brightened by fire points of leashed excitement.

"Simpson, this may be your last night on earth."

Hardship had quenched much of the cowman's resolve. He spoke now in a low held voice: "For God's sake, Gorman, let my boy go. He's done you no harm."

"Nor will he, Simpson."

"They won't bargain with you, Gorman, you're an outlaw. Let Dade go and keep me. I promise you I'll stand up in his place."

Simpson's pleading reached Lee. He writhed under its clearly audible anguish and watched his father.

Uriah turned away, looked up where Zeke was coming back toward them and beyond, where the sleeping soldier was lying darkly still in the dust of the roadside gutter.

"Good," Uriah said. "Now come along."

They clumped after him as far as the preëmpted law office that had become emergency head-quarters for the soldiers, and when Uriah lifted the latch and inched inside, they followed.

A spatter of lamp glow struck them all and bounced off. Their shadows on the back wall were enormous. A soldier clerk cocked back with his feet on a desk opened his eyes, wide. He made no other show of awareness except that his face went white.

Uriah spoke into this look of incredulity and quickening fear. "Where's your officer?"

"Asleep."

The reply was a low whisper. Another time the soldier's expression would have been funny; now it wasn't. Uriah moved silently around the desk and disarmed the soldier, who took his feet off the desk and brought his chair down gently, still staring at the bulging eyes.

"In that room?" Uriah asked, with a head nod toward a closed door.

"Yes, sir."

"George, go fetch him . . . and be sure you take his weapons."

Dobkins went through the door and shortly they heard gruff profanity coming into the hush. It grew briefly louder, then went silent. Moments later a thin man clad only in soiled full-length underwear appeared. He looked at Uriah, at the others, at the Simpsons bound at the wrists and haggard. Through the mists of dullness came quick understanding. "Who are you?" he asked, although he knew who they were. "What the hell do you mean coming in here like this?"

"My name is Uriah Gorman," Gorman answered with an urgent ringing in his voice. "I'm leader of the sheepmen. This here is Charles Simpson and his son Dade. They are my hostages."

"Hostages," the officer repeated. "You damned old Rebel you. Those men were abducted and you're the leader of nothing. You're an outlaw, proclaimed so by law. Now if you know what's . . ."

Uriah interrupted harshly. "I didn't come here to argue," he said, keeping his voice down with a struggle. "I came here to offer terms." He paused. The officer's face twitched, his eyes blinked rapidly but he did not speak. "We are entitled to equal range rights with the cowmen under the law. We demand them. In exchange for that to which we have full right . . . and for your protection in seeing that the free-graze law is upheld . . . and your protection of all sheepmen . . . we will give up our hostages and stop fighting."

Uriah stood, giant-like, in the middle of the room. Behind him, also filling the space of two ordinary men, were Lee and Zeke. Less impressive except for his bared hand gun and beard-stubbled grimness, George Dobkins stood fast in dripping shadows. The Simpsons were staring steadily at the weather-beaten officer and he, in turn, did not take his eyes from Uriah's bitter-set face and eyes of green ice.

"Gorman, you're crazy. By God, you've got to be to bust in here like this, and make such a tomfool demand." Each word fell bell-clear in the deep stillness. "You're a murderer. There are a dozen warrants out for you. Over three hundred men are hunting your band. You can't be serious in this, man."

"I was never more serious." Uriah's jaw clamped closed. "Zeke," he ordered after a moment of thought, "take this man back to his room. Have him get dressed. Fully dressed in his uniform, then bring him back."

They waited. Uriah turned and fastened a deliberate stare upon the shaken orderly. He seemed to be considering something, then he looked away and his shoulders drooped a little.

Zeke reëntered the small room behind the

officer. Uriah looked long at the smooth blue uniform, at the encrusted shoulder straps, at the girt-saber and its handsome sword knots glowing golden in the light. He brought his eyes back to the captain's face with an effort, and those behind him could not see. Only Zeke, looking fully at his father over the captain's shoulder, saw the surface lights of madness lambent in the lusterless green stare.

"Your name, sir," Uriah asked in a tone of sifting ashes. "Your name and outfit."

"Captain Gower Hardin, Fourth Cavalry."

"Captain Hardin you have our terms. Do you accept them or not?"

The officer's eyes were dryly staring, round with comprehension and incredulity. "And if I don't?" he asked.

"Then I'll have no choice. You are an enemy. I cannot leave you alive in my rear and you know that."

The quick explosion of two voices simultaneously filled the room. One was from the clerk orderly, who sprang up now. The other belonged to Lee. His prevailed; it was loudest.

"Paw! For God's sake what are you doing?"

"This!" Uriah roared in his thunderous voice so that echoes crashed throughout the room.

It happened too fast. There were only splinters of things to see, to be forever imbedded in seven minds. The foot-long Dragoon pistol came up and tilted back. Uriah cocked it. The officer turned white to the eyes. He stared at the gun. His orderly would have sprung forward but George Dobkins's gun crunched against his skull and he crumpled to the floor with a gentle swishing sound.

Zeke was moving clear when Uriah fired. His mouth was wide open. One of Hardin's upflung arms struck Zeke as the officer was flung backward in his fall. Before the sound had fully died, Dobkins was keening in a shaken voice.

"We got to get out of here. We got to run for it. Hurry!"

Lee turned toward the door and stumbled. Someone caught his arm in an iron grasp and gave him a savage push through. It was Uriah. Behind him Zeke was punching the Simpsons along. No one said anything but over the sound of their pounding boots arose a sudden cry.

At the entrance to the dogtrot Uriah paused to await the Simpsons and Zeke. He still held his pistol. When the Simpsons came up, he raised it but Zeke was too fast. He struck the gun aside, grabbed Uriah's shoulder, and hurled him into the narrow passageway. With a shout and a toss of his head Zeke told the Simpsons to run. They ran, even if awkwardly because their arms were bound behind them, but desperately and as rapidly as they could.

Beyond the dogtrot and moving restlessly in the

darkness, the others sat their saddles with drawn guns. They had heard the shot that killed Gower Hardin. Kant U'Ren leaned low and held Uriah's reins out. Uriah did not take them at once. Pete Amaya urged his horse up toward Lee and waited for the younger man to mount. His round dark face was glistening with excitement.

Lee, Zeke, and George Dobkins got quickly astride. Uriah shucked out the spent casing from his pistol and reloaded it. Then he faced the others.

"Which of you knows where Bob Ander lives?" he asked in a voice as emotionless and dry as a breath of air among cornhusks.

Lee leaned from the saddle, sheet-white and staring. "That was murder. You can't do it again."

Chapter Ten

After Lee's outburst there was silence. None of them knew where Town Marshal Ander lived, or, if they did know, they did not say. They were vastly more interested in the sounds around them of a rousing populace.

Finally Kant U'Ren said: "Come on, Uriah, let's go. We can get Ander another time."

"You fool," Uriah stormed, making no move to mount up. "If we don't kill him now, we may never get him. They'll be after us like a pack of hounds come dawn."

"U'Ren's right," a shadowy rider said, shortening his reins. "Come on, Uriah."

The elder Gorman still hesitated.

Then Lee spoke over the sudden burst of excited gabbling around front. "He doesn't care about lives . . . he wants to kill."

Pedro Amaya, farthest back and facing an alley, made a quavering cry of alarm. "They are coming. They have lanterns and they are coming up this alleyway."

Uriah mounted, then, but he still did not lead them away. He sat his saddle, gauging the distance of the mob and its numbers. In his mind thoughts ran together to form a dark beauty from violence; he could charge into that crowd and shoot down maybe ten of them. They wouldn't give quarter— then they deserved none. Hurried words from the warp of his mind, from his secret soul, made him temporarily oblivious to peril.

"We've got rights!" he roared suddenly. "We ask no more'n we deserve."

"You'll get it, too," Kant U'Ren told him harshly, "if you sit here much longer."

"Shut your damned mouth!" he roared at the half-breed. "Cowards, I'm surrounded by cowards!"

Lee flung his horse between his father and the oncoming mob with its roaring malevolent sound and its highly held and swinging lanterns. His face was split by a ghastly expression and his hair stood up like Uriah's hair, like snakes caught up and writhing.

"Paw, there's mounted men amongst 'em!"

"So I see," said Uriah in a cold and detached manner. He reined around Lee and started toward the mob with his hand gun ready.

It was big Zeke who swung up, grabbed Uriah's reins, and yanked back so abruptly that Uriah was thrown forward in the saddle and nearly tumbled to the ground. His head snapped around and hot eyes grew still on his eldest.

"Scared to die like a man are you, Ezekiel?"

"There's no call to die," retorted his angered son. "Lee, take the others and ride out the way we came in. Go on!"

Zeke let go his father's reins. They were close now, glaring across at one another. "You undid what little good we might have done here tonight," the son said savagely. "Now come on. Look there . . . at least ten of 'em got rifles and horses."

Uriah looked. His face cleared suddenly, became stark and iron-like again. "To the east," he said brusquely. "Ride east and follow me."

They went clattering across the summer-hard ground with a sound like thunder in their wake. Rode swiftly and unerringly back through the rows of houses, some lit now, and Uriah didn't draw up for many miles, until the men called to him that their horses were faltering. By then they were far off and well clear of any pursuit.

Lee thought his father had gone from one extreme to the other, from wanting to fight the whole of Union City to wanting to flee out of Wyoming itself. He drew up and looked around. He counted shadows—eight. He counted again. There should have been ten.

Kant U'Ren eased down beside him. "There's no more coming," he said. "Two split off miles back. I saw them go. Good riddance." U'Ren started forward where Pete and Uriah were talking. He said over his shoulder: "They ain't got the chance of a snowball in hell. The law'll be after 'em like the devil after a crippled saint." He laughed, a musical, diminishing sound as he rode away.

Uriah led them south now. Steadily south until the rolling uplands of Cottonwood Creek were nigh. There, he went in among trees along a hogback and dismounted.

The ground was soft and damp from leaf mold. There was some grass for the animals but not much. Beyond, down the southwesterly slope, the creek was visible, an oily black in the paling moonlight. Pete Amaya, seeking good feed for his mount, came upon a buck and shot it. Uriah cursed and railed, until Pete came back with the meat, then he went silent. They made a fire, cooked venison, and ate it. There was neither coffee nor whiskey but there did not have to be. Eight shrunken bellies swelled to bursting and the effect was the same. They became less

154

morose, less rebellious in thought and expression.

Uriah ate standing, listening, head cocked in that familiar stance they had come to know him by. Wolf-wary and Indian-like. Then suddenly he left them, walking southerly through the tangle of trees, softened by the mist and silent. None of them looked around to watch him go.

George Dobkins moved over where Zeke was lying full-length on his saddle blanket. He was smoking, something he rarely did, and watching the dawn mist swirl up from the creek. Dobkins sat down and sucked his teeth for a while before speaking.

"That was a bad thing back there," he said.

"Yeah."

"If we had any sympathizers before, we ain't got 'em now."

"I suppose not."

Lee came up to them and sank down. His face was haggard beneath its coating of grime and stubble. His eyes sought his brother's gaze briefly, then moved away. Dobkins studied the younger man from beneath his hat brim. There was a great layer of unhappiness on the younger man's face— a weakness he thought—but he said no more of what was on his mind. After a time he left the brothers alone, went out to check his horse. He did not mean for his animal to be weak when the time came to run for it.

Lee watched Dobkins go. Zeke did not look

away from the treetops nor did he blink or act as though he knew Lee was there beside him.

After a long interval Zeke said: "I reckon you didn't see his face back there, did you?"

"Paw's?"

"Yeah. I was across the room from him . . . behind the officer. I saw it real good. Real good."

"Well, I was behind him."

"I know. Too bad. You should've seen it, Lee."

Lee knew. It wasn't necessary for him to have seen his father's face, at all. "Zeke, you were right . . . that going to Union City was the craziest thing he ever did."

"I figured he was going to do something like that. I figured for a while he was fighting for our rights on the range. You know . . . like we all figured."

"No," the younger man said. "I knew different. I told you so after what happened at XIH."

"He's crazy," said Zeke flatly. "All right. I see that. I believe it now. But tell me . . . just what in hell is in his head? Doesn't he know they'll surround us now and run us down for what he did at Union City?" Zeke got up on one elbow and looked at his brother. "Hell, we couldn't even surrender now, boy. Not even if we wanted to."

Lee was looking to the north. There was nothing in this conversation that held him. In his mind he'd said it all before. Northerly was the Foster place.

Zeke watched his brother's face a moment, then grunted and lay back again. In a dead voice he said: "Forget it, Lee. Forget you ever touched her. Damned small chance you'll ever see her again."

"Zeke . . . ?"

"No," he answered before the question was asked. "Not a chance, boy, and you know it. Like I said . . . forget her. You wouldn't get halfway there before some damned posse'd have you swinging from an oak limb."

It was the truth and Lee knew it, but its full impact and starkness became evident only when it was put into words. He turned toward the cooking fire, dying now, and went low against the ground. The others were sleeping flat in the dirt with twitching arms and legs. Around them the misted world was brightening opaquely. He had just closed his eyes, it seemed, when Uriah came back, light-footed, all tall and angular with shadows around him, and roused them up.

"They're hunting us hard," he said.

A shapeless form struggled upright. "You saw them?"

Uriah hunkered by the fire with a headshake. He began throwing dirt on the flames. "I didn't see them, no. I went back a mile or so and put my ear to the ground. They're riding, boys, they're riding. I heard them."

Dobkins and another man exchanged a secret look. Around them grew a stirring. Men got to their feet numbly. Dobkins went over to stand behind their leader. "Uriah," he asked, "what ailed you back there? You were fixing to ride right into them."

Lee got to his feet tensed to leap between them. He mentally cursed Dobkins's foolishness. But Uriah didn't explode, didn't even turn to face Dobkins when he answered because in his mind a voice was speaking and he harkened to it. *You've led them, Uriah. You've led them to triumph and there is a wealth of weariness in you. You've led them and shielded them and saved them and now you're dog-tired. You're old. Amethyst is gone. A harlot robbed your youngest of his soul. Your eldest is drawing apart from you. . . . The others will, too, in time.*

A darkness bowed him under and rode his spirit. "I do what I know is best," he told George Dobkins. "I am not new at this."

Lee, listening, felt his father's words ring in his heart—heavy words, as heavy as stone. He was tense all over, taut as a bowstring.

"Sit down, boy," his brother said from the ground. "Leave 'em be."

But Lee did not relax until Dobkins and another man went out to look to the horses and Uriah took out his case knife and worried off big mouthfuls of dripping deer meat. Then he sank back down. Beside him Zeke was already asleep, his breath a rhythmic bubbling in the damp stillness.

Uriah did not rouse them again until the shimmer of breaking day whirled the mist. Then he ordered them to saddle up. "We dassn't stay long in one place," he said. They moved. Their legs dragged and their fingers were clumsy with cinches, with bits and headstalls and blankets. He led them cautiously across the open slope toward the creek, then through the unfamiliar green screening of willows and tules close by the water. An uneasy wind strode down the land behind them shredding the mist, then it died and the only sound was of hoofs sucking up loudly from the mud.

Lee smelled the air. A hot day was ahead, a good summer day. For a moment a droplet of hope enlivened his spirit; he liked the heat, the sun, the strong heavy air of Wyoming summer days. He loved summer the best. It had unrestrained color. The tang of wind at dawn, the savor of richness, of growth and fecundity . . .

Uriah made for a little land swell and halted there to peer out under the lifting mist. "Look there," he said with sudden sharpness, his face darkening, turning evil and hating again.

Lee tugged back to stop, brought harshly back to reality with a start by the thinness of his father's tone.

Little parties of horsemen, bunched up and scattered out not more than ten to a band, were criss-crossing the land. *Like soldiers,* thought Lee.

There's some kind of a plan behind the way they're doing that. He watched several clutches of the riders cross the creek far north of them at spaced intervals. Not a tree or willow clump was left unscrutinized.

A cadaverous raider with a bony face and deep-sunken eyes spoke beside him. "Like old times," he said, watching ahead. "Skirmish order."

George Dobkins, sitting his saddle like a statue, nodded. "Ander was a soldier. I've heard that said many times."

Uriah announced: "We'd best get moving. Westerly now, boys, and take care. They are a long way off but there'll be others and maybe closer. Keep to cover."

Lee twisted his head. *Keep to cover? How? Where?* When they left the creek, they also left the cover. There was too much open country around them now and with the fog lifting they could not go far undetected. His throat tightened and his mouth became dry.

Uriah led them back to the creek and along it for a mile, then, where the crumbling banks swerved easterly toward Union City, he paused only for a moment then pushed on.

Lee looked longingly toward the mountains, westerly. They knew every cranny of those hills, every hide-out and dark cañon. The cowmen were there, yes, but they did not know the mountains well. He straightened in the saddle. Beside him

Pete Amaya's raffish grin shone with bright confidence.

"Your Paw's crazy like a fox," the Mexican said. He lifted an arm and flagged easterly with it. "Who will think to look for us at Union City?"

Lee's sweeping glance showed him instantly that they were indeed heading toward Union City. In a strangling voice he said: "You fool . . ."

"No, no, *amigo*. He's right. You are young. You are inexperienced. You do not know about these things. Look, there are men all over the range looking for us." Amaya's black eyes danced. "They have stripped their settlement bare to chase outlaws. *Amigo*, they will not expect us to get behind them."

"We can't," Lee said sharply. "We can't get behind them, you fool. Didn't you see the way they're combing the prairie? Besides, we got no friends at Union City. If we get there, we'll never be able to get away again."

But Pedro Amaya had blind allegiance. It was perhaps all he had besides inherent cruelty but it was enough. He did not believe Uriah could be beaten, let alone outthought. He urged his horse away from Lee's side, still wearing his solid smile.

Uriah led them craftily back and forth in a way that kept them hidden by rolls of land or fingerlings of timber and brush until they were less than three miles from Union City. Behind them, still visible on their flank, was the creek. Then he stopped and let them all cluster up before he pointed ahead with a rigid arm. Lee had to move his horse around Kant U'Ren, sitting stiffly in the saddle, rifle athwart his thighs, to see.

There was a strung-out blue line of soldiers moving at a brisk trot toward the village. Bright sunlight winked off shiny accoutrements and along the burning edge of drawn sabers.

U'Ren grunted. "It's like we was already in the damned town," he said. "What in hell d'you expect they're up to?"

It was Zeke who told them. "Look north of town there," he said, "and you'll see plain enough even from here. That's a freshly made scaffolding there."

Lee looked as did the others. The distance was great but not too great. New lumber bone-white in the sparkling brightness stood out where a gibbet had been constructed. It was long, long enough to hang four men at a time.

Said a hoarse voice: "They got Fawcett and Bachelor and . . ."

"Be quiet!" Uriah ordered, his face turned iron-like, acid-etched, and bleak. "They likely got nobody. They're just praying they might."

"That prayer'll likely get answered, too," U'Ren said.

Uriah turned a flinty stare on him, but U'Ren did not notice. He was staring far ahead, his dark, lean face gone hard and impassive, his thin lips lying relaxed and closed in thoughtfulness. "Well," he finally added, "no sense in going closer now."

Uriah concurred but not right away. He continued to stare at the gibbet as unaware as the rest of them that horsemen had appeared on a far-off knoll, had drawn up suddenly, and were studying them from a distance.

Not until a fluting cry quivered like quicksilver in the fresh warmth did Uriah jerk around. Then he saw them spurring down from the knob, guns bared and horses plunging on loose reins.

"Come on, boys!" he called, and spun his mount downslope toward the creek. They drew weapons and followed him in a rush. Lee was the last man. He sat a moment, staring. One of the posse's leaders was familiar to him. It was Lew Foster, Ann's father. Then he fled after the others and overtook Zeke who was hanging back, waiting for him.

They heard the crackle of gunfire coming from the swale behind but were protected from pursuit by the land swell. Zeke craned for a backward look. He was worried. Gunfire this day would be heard a long way off. As far as Union City probably since the air was that clear and conductive.

At the creek's bank Uriah swung on his excited horse. His awry beard jutted and his flaming eyes burned with excitement he made no attempt to control. "Across!" he cried. "Across and ambush 'em on the far side."

They plunged into the water, got across, and followed the old man's example of dismounting. After the horse holders led the animals away there were only six of them.

From the creekbank, Zeke called out: "Twelve by my count! That's Lew Foster's buckskin in the lead."

"Come here, Zeke. The rest of you spread out. Let 'em get into the water before you shoot. Lee . . . you owe Foster something. Kill him." Uriah's mouth hung slack in long silence while he glared at his youngest. "Kill him, boy!"

They scattered into the willows, flattened in low places, and pushed their rifles out with sweaty hands. They could plainly see the bunched-up riders advancing from the northeast toward the creek. They came sweeping down the slow-depending slope and suddenly opened fire.

"Hold," Uriah commanded sternly, his voice calm now and low. "Don't shoot yet . . . not till they're in the water. Then aim low, boys . . . belly-low, and don't miss 'em, the murderers!"

The riders broke and scattered. A burly man astride a magnificent black gelding flung up an arm, and shouted: "They ain't beyond the creek! Be careful now . . ."

As well try to stem a flood. The posse men had

been long at this search. They were not to be stopped now. Four of them let off keening Indian yells and raced recklessly for the silver roll of water.

On Lee's right Kant U'Ren snugged back his rifle, traced out the shifting shape of a rider down his barrel, and squeezed off a shot. Horse and man went down in a crashing tumult. Behind them three others screamed at their mounts and sought to check the headlong rush. As they were fighting around, U'Ren levered up another bullet and raised his head. He was smiling. He had no intention of firing again.

Across the creek posse men stopped beyond range and milled around. Closer, a solitary horseman sat motionlessly, staring at the willow tangle. To Lee's eyes he was elusively familiar.

"Who is that feller off by himself, there?" he called to Zeke.

The older brother answered without taking his eyes off the milling men beyond. "Garner. That U.S. marshal from Denver. I recognize his horse."

Uriah's voice rose in scorn. "They're sending back for help. Two to one, and they're going for help."

It was true. A doubled-over rider was spurring rapidly back over the land swell in the direction of Union City.

Lee watched him a moment, cocked a glance at the sun overhead, and got up on to one knee.

165

"He'll bring back the soldiers, Paw. Let's get out of here."

Bullets drove him flat again and Uriah did not answer. The posse men were afoot now and advancing in a zigzag run toward the east bank of the creek. They had detailed horse holders to take their animals farther up the slope and out of harm's way.

"Now!" Uriah cried sharply. "Now! Before they get to the willows!"

The sudden fire brought down two posse men. One fell like a lightning-struck tree and did not move again. The second man writhed upon the tender grass and screamed. His companions wilted under the steady volleys. They looked right and left for leadership, then broke and fled back the way they had come. Lee saw Burt Garner running after them loosely and slowly, as though ashamed. Halfway up the slope was the unmistakable figure of Lew Foster. He was well in the lead now, as he had also been far back during the earlier charge.

"Hold your fire!" Uriah commanded. He had to repeat it twice, louder each time before Pete Amaya pushed his rifle aside to peer through the willows at their routed foemen. He probably never did hear Uriah's order. He was grinning happily.

"Bring up the horses!"

The men got to their feet and waited. When the

animals appeared, Uriah made no move toward them. He was standing erectly with his rifle butt down and gazing up the far slope. "Like quail," he said, in the first soft voice those around him had heard him use in days. "Like quail, boys." He did not smile at them but there were no longer shadows in his gaze. "If that's how they took this country from the Indians, then the Indians must've been pretty sorry fighting men."

No one looked at Kant U'Ren. They had forgotten the half-blood. But it did not matter. U'Ren was openly smiling.

Zeke studied the distant posse men through slitted lids. His face was composed, too, but thoughtfully so. "Now where?" he asked of his father.

"Don't worry. Just mount up and follow me. There's a sight more to this than just running all the time."

"Yes," said Amaya. "We win each time we meet them." He turned a guileless eye on Lee. "You see?"

Lee made no reply. He got astride and followed the others away from the willow bank, rode half turned in the saddle to watch their enemies.

There was no pursuit.

Kant U'Ren rode beside Zeke. "They're watching. They won't try to stop us," he said.

Zeke lifted his shoulders and let them fall. "I thought you were smarter than Amaya, U'Ren. I figured you for a man who's seen things like this before."

"I have."

"Then why don't you use your damned head. They're not scared of us."

"No? Then why're they letting us ride off 'thout even trying to stop us?"

"Because," answered Zeke, "they're waiting for the Army. When the soldiers come up, they'll come after us ten to one and maybe more. By this time tomorrow I think you might get a chance to see whether we've whipped 'em or not. Whether they're scared of us or not."

Chapter Eleven

But Zeke had calculated without the craftiness of his father. Wild in the head, old Uriah might be but he was no fool. He led them straight for the hills until the sun dipped and sank far off, then he slowed and they ambled along with the blue east behind them, making them vague and shadowy and dim to the eye, and after full dusk fell he turned around without a word and headed back for the creek.

There was a ripple of fear among them, a murmur of doubt, but they followed. Uriah's hold was on them all, even the disillusioned, the ones like Lee who rode now without speaking or even looking at his companions. He was sick with fatigue. There was a numb, oblivious look in his eyes as if he no longer cared. Behind him came big Zeke, chewing venison and staring at his father's back. Behind Zeke rode U'Ren. It mattered very little to him, either. He was shrewd without being intelligent and that made him a fatalist. Even Pete Amaya, farther back still, knew fear at first, but as always with him, blind allegiance triumphed. He, too, was chewing deer meat as he slumped along.

When they had covered nearly a mile there came to them a feeling, a quivering in the night stillness that, communicating itself to them, passed along the column. They sensed danger from the very darkness that was their ally—a sudden alarm in the atmosphere some way. Uriah drew up, sniffing and listening, a shaggy old sheepdog of a man gauntly straining. Then all their minds merged into one thought and there was a general stir of bodies—pursuit.

North of them a ways came the faint but growing rumble of a large mounted force moving swiftly to the west. They listened with held breath, with stilled jaws and widened eyes. The clatter grew louder, louder, then it began to diminish, to flee away from them toward the mountains, and in the gut of each outlaw the knots lessened, leaving behind a thoroughly drained and weakened feeling. Only Uriah seemed unaffected. Without a word he shortened his reins, turned his back on them, and pushed on to the creek.

They splashed across in a bunch as silent as only tense men can be. Then Uriah swung northward a little and after a while Lee's head came up. He turned from an orienting study of the landfall to an equally as puzzled study of his father's back. A rider edged up and bumped stirrups with him. It was Zeke. His face held an irony; there was no puzzlement. He was too like Uriah. He knew where they were going. He thought he knew why, too.

When they topped out on the gravelly ridge Uriah stopped. Below them, lying square and soft-limned by moonlight, lay the Foster place. The men crowded up close. Like Uriah they knew whose ranch this was. They also remembered with vividness, Lew Foster leading the cowmen against them at the creek.

"Zeke, you and the rest stay here and watch." Uriah's shadowed eyes swept past Lee to Kant U'Ren and Pete Amaya. "You boys come with me."

"Paw!"

Uriah ignored the quick cry of his youngest. He looked hard at Zeke. "See that *he* stays with you."

That was all.

Amaya and U'Ren rode forward. They followed Uriah down the hill.

In Lee the forces of desperation and horror came up strong. "He'll kill 'em, Zeke. Listen, I got to go."

"You stay, boy."

"But, Zeke!"

A hard headshake. "No, he won't kill her. No matter what he thinks . . . he won't kill a woman."

"He'll kill Lew. He killed that officer, Zeke."

The older brother looked broodingly down the hill. There was nothing to see, no sound or movement anywhere. He thought it very likely that Uriah would kill Lew Foster, but in searching his mind he could find no sorry feeling for that.

"Zeke . . . !"

"No! You stay!"

Zeke did not look at Lee. It was George Dobkins's voice that came next, soft but sharp in the gloom. "Hold it, Lee. Think . . ."

Dobkins's hand was holding fast to the younger man's gun hand, forcing it down, down, away from the weapon Lee had clutched.

"One shot'll bring the whole damned countryside down on us, boy. Think . . ."

From the pinched-down little valley below there came lamplight but that was all. There was no shot. Dobkins's fingers loosened and finally drew away, but the man kept his eyes turned fully on the brothers. A lantern came from the house. It bobbed toward the barn. From the hilltop it was impossible to see who carried it, or if he was alone or with others.

Zeke dismounted and stamped his feet. Several others did the same. Dobkins did not turn away

171

from Lee, and the youngest Gorman stared toward the lighted barn without moving until the lantern went out and shortly afterward the sound of horses moving uphill came scratchily through the silence.

They were all mounted and ready when Uriah herded his new hostages among them. Lew Foster's hip holster was empty; his arms were bound behind him. He was sweating and badly frightened. Most of the sheepmen looked away from his face. They were embarrassed for him. Neither Paxton Clement nor Charles Simpson had shown fear, once.

Kant U'Ren and Pete Amaya herded the second hostage toward Lee. They were both smiling, Amaya the widest, as though bringing Ann to her lover was his exclusive notion, his contribution to a *companero*'s happiness.

"Let's go!" Uriah called, taking the lead and pushing on through the darkness.

There was no time for talk. Ann looked once searchingly into Lee's face and that was all. Kant U'Ren rode behind her, black eyes saturnine, flat face softened by the faintest of smiles. Lee took the shank from U'Ren. The half-breed relinquished it without a word. They rode together like that with Lee leading her horse, keeping it abreast of his own Grulla, silent, full of longing, full of hunger but silent.

When they swung easterly, George Dobkins

asked Uriah where they were going now. The answer came coldly: "I make few plans ahead. Life is how you find it." After that no one broke the silence.

Uriah led them with the guile of Indian wisdom, with still watchfulness and cold implacability guiding his every step, his every move. When they came at last to the final thicket before the brushed-off prairie beyond the southernmost shacks of Union City, none was surprised. They had all long since divined his course if not his purpose.

He made them all dismount and check their weapons. It was a wasted moment. For the last half mile every hand had been closed around a pistol or a rifle and every mouth had been dry and every mind had been pulling away from what each man was afraid lay ahead. Still, none of them challenged Uriah. Not even Zeke. With several, fatigue and bewilderment had dulled thoughts, and with others, like U'Ren and the Mexican, there was a shrug, an indifference—even a tiny belief that Uriah could pull it off—whatever he had in mind. But George Dobkins and Lee had no such illusions and the older man looked around for the wispy man he had talked guardedly with before. He could not make him out in the black light.

Uriah had them leave their horses tied. He did not detail anyone to hold the horses. There were only eight of them as it was. This was his second mistake—his first was to lead them there at all.

"Forward," he called softly, and led them first to a stinking sumpage hole where green scum and bones of animals lay. There was a rank growth to hide in but the stench was overpowering. Lee saw Ann's silent distress and would have untied her hands but Kant U'Ren, crouching on her far side, stopped him with a scowl and headshake. Then Uriah's voice caught their attention.

"You all know where the jailhouse is. That's our destination. Whoever they got in there, we'll get out."

Dobkins spoke up in quick protest. "But, Uriah, dammit all . . . them fellers deserted us."

"It makes no difference. They're sheepmen and, by God, we cleave to ours like the cowmen cleave to theirs." The insistent low voice trailed off for a moment, then rose again more strongly than before. "Besides, we need four more guns, boys. We need 'em bad, and I figure those men in there know by now there's no way to escape from this fight except by winning it. They won't try to run off again."

Dobkins licked dry lips and closed them, tight. Like the others he looked ahead to the nearest shacks and beyond where Union City's solitary wide thoroughfare ran arrow-straight due north and south. There were many lights and some noise, but not much activity. Unseen but starkly etched in each mind's eye was the green-pine scaffolding northerly beyond town. It could strangle four men at a time.

Close ahead a fat woman came to a door and cast out slops from a tin wash basin. At another shack a man walked out into the night's warmth and looked skyward. He was smoking a pipe from which irregular puffs of smoke rose straight up, and he was shirtless, his thick chest and corded arms encased in long summer underwear. He scratched his belly and smoked and studied the clear-curving night. They thought he would never go back indoors but he finally did, slowly, seemingly reluctantly. When the door closed after him, the night was empty again. It belonged to those crouching in wait by the sump hole.

"Quiet now," Uriah said, unwinding stiffly from his crouch, using his rifle for leverage. "Don't make a sound. We'll work along the back of town a ways until we're close by the jailhouse."

Zeke waited to speak until Uriah was passing. "Leave the Fosters here, Paw. Gag 'em and tie 'em to a tree. They'll be in the way."

Uriah, moving now, eyes dancing first one way then the other, watching the shacks, the town, the north-south roadway, answered shortly. "They're hostages. If we run into trouble, we'll use 'em to bargain with. Now come along . . . quit talking and fetch the prisoners along. If they make a sound, slit their gullets. Hurry . . ."

In places they had to crawl because there was no

175

cover but darkness. There was broken pottery as white as bones but sharper, and débris of many kinds. A man tore his shirt and drew blood and cursed softly. Uriah hissed angrily at him. Sweat dripped off their faces. Beside Lee, Ann Foster was ashen. Her lips were tightly closed. She did not look at him, not even when he put out a hand to touch her cheek. Lew Foster was with Pete Amaya. Like Ann he looked stonily ahead, pale to the eyes.

Lee kept worrying about retreat. Afoot, he felt helpless, naked. If there was serious trouble, escape back the way they had come to where the animals were tied would be impossible. Half the village would be shooting at them. By tossing his head he flung droplets of sweat off his chin.

Back a ways Kant U'Ren said: "We're getting close."

It was an unnecessary remark. Ahead of them, beyond where Uriah crouched, lay a dusty strip of earth. It separated them from the two houses that flanked the jailhouse on either side. Lee went flat beside Ann with his pounding heart. She turned, looked him squarely in the eye, and spoke in a whisper. Her first words this night.

"You'll never make it, Lee. Your father's wrong. Everyone isn't out hunting you. Not after what you did to Captain Hardin."

Lee would have replied but Dobkins spoke up sharply to Uriah. "There's a rider coming down the alleyway," he said, and every face lifted a little to strain for the image.

The horseman was riding loosely, tiredly. He was coming along the alley from the west, probably from one of the posses that were out. They watched him approach, then turn into the rear of a livery barn before he was close enough to see them. Lee looked around for Zeke. The older brother was sinking down again and the way he did it showed immeasurable relief. He did not see Lee watching him.

Lee squirmed closer to Ann, felt the warmth of her leg and hip. "Ann, it was the old man killed that soldier. Zeke tried to stop him. I would have, too, only it happened too fast."

She had her gaze riveted to Uriah's raw-boned crouching silhouette. She kept silent.

Pete Amaya whispered aloud: "He give up maybe. He got tired and come back." He meant the horseman.

Uriah threw up an arm for silence, then began maneuvering closer to the livery barn's wide rear opening. They all followed him as silently as Indians until the broad alleyway beyond was visible, with its guttering lanterns and moving men. Uriah kept his hard vigil. He saw the weary rider talking to other men who broke up shortly and went yelling for still others out into the far roadway. Into all this Uriah read meaning, for he nodded his head up and down.

"He come back to tell them something. They've found where we had a camp, I expect. They're going to make up another posse."

They remained, motionless and watching, until the fresh riders came together, milled briefly around the tired man who was mounted now on a fresh horse, then they all loped vigorously northward.

When the last sound had faded, Uriah stood upright boldly and said: "Now! Now!"

Lee got up with the rest of them. There was dust all over him. When he slapped his clothing it squirted outward in thick clouds. He moved ahead with the others, following Uriah, and like the others he was watchful.

Uriah led them noiselessly straight up to the strap-steel door of the jailhouse's rear exit before he looked back. They were all there. All tightly wound and shaken but persevering now that they had followed him this far. He lowered his head, pressed an ear to the door a moment, then rapped sharply on the panel with his rifle butt. A hollow echo came back muted by massive mud walls.

"Who's there?"

"Ander," Uriah growled. "Open up."

There came a sliding, a creaking, and the door swung slightly inward. Uriah hurled himself against it, and as far back as Lee stood, could be heard the grunt and gasp of the man inside. Pete Amaya whipped past Lee with great speed.

Wraith-like he got inside with his cocked revolver. They all pushed in quickly and George Dobkins eased the door closed after them.

Inside, it was cool and nearly dark and with a sour smell to the air. They mobbed up close around the frightened jailer. He was a fat man and his mouth was still contorted from the pain where the door had slammed into his paunch. His blue eyes widened, showed pure panic in their depths, then glazed over. He was near to fainting dead away.

"Don't yell out," Uriah commanded. "Zeke, take his gun."

Out of nowhere a knife appeared blurring with movement. It sank swiftly, and into the stunned silence they all heard it ripping flesh, grating past bone. Then the jailer fell in a heap, his mouth working soundlessly, his body writhing.

"U'Ren!"

The half-breed moved back and looked down. His knife was scarlet and shiny with blood. Across from him Lee half turned, disbelieving. It was Uriah standing like stone, looking down at spreading scarlet, who spoke then, closing his mind against this murder and reverting to his own ways.

"Zeke, slip up and see if there's anyone else in the front office. Kant, you stay back here by the alley entrance. Bar that door again."

He started forward after Zeke, turned once

impatiently to watch the others step high over the dead jailer, then resumed his way.

Lee, frozen to the ground with Ann at his side, gulped for air, for relief from the internal constricting band behind his belt that would not slacken. A burning flared in his head. He didn't hear the loud, high call of a name up ahead until Ann's fingers closed over his arm and drew him along.

"He says to get the keys off the jailer, Lee. Lee . . . do you hear me?" She got the keys herself and forced them into his hand. They moved around the corpse with only U'Ren's thin scornful look to see their paleness.

Beyond the marshal's office was a second door, flung back. Through it came voices raised shrilly in relief, in fright and excitement. Uriah jerked away the key ring from Lee and gave him a bleak stare before pushing through where Harold Baker and Joseph Fawcett were straining against the bars, keening the same words over and over. Lee did not understand them, nor did Ann or Uriah until Zeke loomed up barring Uriah's way with his massiveness.

"Paw . . ."

"No time for talk. Get out of my way, boy."

"You got to listen, dammit."

"Ezekiel, we ain't got the time!"

He would have brushed past but Zeke's big arm shot out, caught him tightly, and shook him bodily.

"It's a trap, damn you! D'you hear me . . . it's a trap!"

They all heard him, even Uriah who wrenched away and took one big stride forward before the full silence of their staring faces stopped him hard. He looked fully at Zeke.

"It's a trap, Paw. They baited us in here."

"They couldn't have," Uriah stormed. He thrust the key ring into Pete Amaya's hand. "Here, let them out." He faced fully around. "They couldn't have baited us, Zeke. How would they know we were coming here?"

Ann Foster shot a flat answer. "Because they know you," she said bitterly, giving Uriah as hard a stare as she got from him. "Because you did it before. You came in here thinking no one would believe you'd dare. That's how."

Uriah's face tightened with care. The color was leached from it. Only his green, feverish stare was the same.

"Uriah!" The cry was full-throated and without caution; every one of them heard and felt its rising, wavering apprehension.

Uriah made no answer. He simply nodded to George Dobkins with the words: "Go see what Kant wants. Hurry now."

But Dobkins was working a key in Joseph Fawcett's cell lock and ignored the order. His hands were shaking badly.

Ann pulled Lee around. They went together to

the rear door where Kant U'Ren was crouching low behind the narrowest of door openings. He beckoned them closer and shifted slightly so they could see into the night.

"Look there, Lee. Out where we was."

Lee moved closer and squinted. Breath whooshed out of him. He did not feel Ann clawing at his back. Without turning and with his mind gone suddenly icily clear, he said to her: "Go get my paw."

When Uriah came he brushed Lee aside and kneeled, stiff and forbidding-looking, the long-barreled Dragoon pistol held tightly. For the space of a heartbeat there was total silence, then Uriah drew back, got erect, and gazed flintily at them. "Seven of them," he said, enunciating very clearly. "It *was* a trap."

U'Ren closed the door, shot the bolt, and leaned back. "They'll have the horses sure's God." He stared hard at Uriah. "How? How did they do it, Uriah? We're holed up here like a bear in his god-damned den."

Joseph Fawcett came up to them, staring into each face. He was gray-faced. "I tried to yell to you, Uriah," he said in a thin, frightened tone. "I tried . . ."

"Joseph, I don't understand."

"They planned it so's if you come back, there'd be fellers all around town. They even had a fake posse made up to ride out and make you think everyone'd left. . . . You walked right into it, Uriah. Right into this god-damned jailhouse and now they got it surrounded."

"They planned it like this?" Uriah asked dazedly, understanding coming very slowly, coming hard and stubbornly.

Fawcett bobbed his head. "Hal and me been listening to them talking about it all day. They got the rifles, too, Uriah."

"Rifles? What rifles you talking about?"

"The ones in the rack in Ander's office. Go look for yourself. They took every weapon and all the shells."

U'Ren spoke a vicious curse and started forward. Uriah's arm shot out and stopped him in mid-stride. His haunted, strange eyes were clear now, and fire-pointed.

"You mind this door, Kant, and remember I'm the one gives orders here."

He flung the half-breed back against the wall. U'Ren's sharp glare dulled. He nodded without malice and moved toward the door. This was what he understood, this was the Uriah Gorman he would obey without question.

Uriah's wrath did not completely die out. He heard others hurrying along the corridor and drew himself up fully erect, waiting until they were all jammed as logs together and barred by his bigness, then he looked upon them with his smoldering wrath. "Go study things out in the roadway," he commanded them. "If there's a way out, it'll be that way."

Lee would have followed the others, would have retreated into the town marshal's office, but for Ann. She blocked his passage where a storeroom lay and steered him into it. Her phlegmaticism was gone now and in its place was a vitality he had never seen in her before.

"Lee, they can't make it across the full width of the roadway. It's crazy to even try it that way."

"Then how?" he cried sharply.

"Probably no way at all," she answered in a voice turning soft and sad. "But if there is a way, it'll be along the back wall as far as the livery barn. In there will be horses."

"I'll tell my paw."

"No, you won't," she snarled at him, moving quickly to block the doorway. "There are ten of them and only two of us. *We* might make it, but *they* never could."

"But, Ann, he's my paw. And there's Zeke . . . and your paw, too."

Small-fisted hands went up against his chest. "I don't care, Lee. I don't care. I'm sick to death of this . . . this hate, this fighting and killing and running. We probably couldn't make it even . . . just the two of us. They'll shoot on sight. I know. But I'd rather be dead with you than go on like this. Lee, look at me. We've got something to live for."

She was clutching his shirt front, shaking him, and her voice was rising. It cracked and fell away to a sob. Her hands dropped down and she cried without making a sound. He folded her against him with pain engulfing him, rocked her gently, oblivious to the sound of pounding boots beyond the storeroom door, deaf to the hoarse cries of his companions as they went scuttling through the building seeking for a way out. Then, when her body was no longer racked with visible anguish, he led her out into the corridor and up toward the marshal's office where most of the others were standing helplessly about, looking at one another. The first voice he heard was Zeke's, rising strong and oddly soft-sounding through the panic.

"How easy they did this. How god-damned easy . . . I reckon Ander out-generalled you, Paw. I've heard he was a soldier in the war."

"Not Bob Ander," Uriah grated harshly. "It was that infernal U.S. marshal from Denver. I sized him up for trouble the first time I set eyes on him at the plateau." He snorted in loud contempt. "Bob Ander wouldn't have the brains *or* the guts."

"Well, it don't matter now. It's done." Zeke was staring blankly at the empty gun rack on the wall. "It's done and here we are sitting in the middle of somebody's trap as neat as greased pigs."

Lee's eyes followed his brother's stare to the empty rack. This, more than anything else, even the frantic gesticulations of Harold Baker and

Joseph Fawcett, brought home to him how their entrapment had been worked out carefully beforehand. He groaned and moved away from Ann toward the barred window where Pete Amaya was crouching, staring out into the hushed and empty roadway, his fixed, happy smile turned gray and strained now, and the dark little hand on his rifle visibly quivering.

"They want a fight," Uriah told them in full throat. "All right! We'll give them no rest!"

Lee turned to look back. Others, too, were staring from haggard faces at Uriah. There he stood, wide-legged, braced forward like one of the old-time Biblical prophets, with his fists clenched and his square jaw set like iron. It was more than Lee could stand. He closed his eyes tightly and faced away.

Chapter Twelve

Beyond the jailhouse windows there was nothing to see. From the vaulted overhead came watery light. It showed empty plank walks, ghostly storefronts, lamp-lit windows. A new silence was everywhere, a boding hush. Union City might have been deserted it was so empty of people, so breathlessly still.

Lee kneeled beside Pete Amaya. Sweat trickled down between his shoulders. The stock of his rifle was slippery, too.

Uriah moved like a caged cat, springy at the knees, head high and canted, eyes moving with liquid flame in their depths. His jaw bulged from the tightness of locked teeth.

Zeke returned from a tour of the windows. He had seen enough blurred movement beyond in the night to know they were surrounded now. He turned to say: "They'll have sent for the soldiers, Paw, and the posses."

"I know, boy, I know."

"Then *do* something!"

"Hush, Zeke."

Uriah crossed to Pete Amaya's side and touched the Mexican with his fingertips. "You're the smallest," he said with his eyes on the empty roadway beyond. "You'll make the least target. Listen to me. We got to have horses. You go out the front door there, zigzag for cover, and hunt us up animals to ride. Try the livery barn or maybe the hitch racks around back of the stores yonder."

Lee arose with Amaya. He looked into his father's face with disbelief. "Paw, he wouldn't get ten feet from that door and you know it."

Uriah did not look away from the roadway at once but his color changed noticeably; dark blood coursed under his cheeks and his eyes came back finally with that terrible wrathful glare, and fixed themselves upon Lee. "Boy," he said in a knife-edged voice, "you been plaguing me about enough lately. You and your Hairston blood . . . your god-damned watery backbone."

Around the still room the others turned. Some stood away from windows, watching. Zeke went fully forward with long strides but he did not get between them. Uriah's arm shot out to stop him.

"Pete'll go," Uriah said in the same edged way. "He's one I can count on."

The little Mexican was looking fully into Uriah's face. He said: "I'll go. It is nothing." No one moved as he padded softly to the door and stopped there, looking back, wearing a weak and crooked little smile. "You will cover me, *señores*?"

Uriah moved forward toward the door. He said: "We'll cover you, Pete, and God go with you." Then he faced the others, still motionless. Each face showing openly the thoughts in every mind. "They can keep up this surround forever. They'll never have to risk a hide to get us. You'd better understand that. They can starve us out, and, when we have to give up, they'll cut us down like dogs when we march out. I know this game. I've seen it played before."

From the corridor's opening Kant U'Ren, recently come forward from the building's rear, nodded approval. "We're more'n likely all dead, anyway," he said into the long silence.

The words went into Lee's skull and rattled there dryly hot and penetrating. He looked for

Ann, saw her standing beside Lew. Then the half-breed spoke again.

"A bullet is better'n a hang rope. Good luck, Pete, you're going to need it."

The Mexican's reply sounded hollow and without conviction. He was still smiling at them all. "I am a lucky man, Kant. I'll make it."

U'Ren nodded gently when he replied: "If I had some money, I'd lay you a bet on how far you get."

Lee saw Uriah stiffen with indignation at this brutal frankness, but he said nothing for the simple reason that there was nothing more to be said. There was not a chance for Pedro Amaya to make it. Not a chance.

George Dobkins shot back the door bolt with damp hands, drew the panel inward silently, and nodded.

Without another look at those behind, standing as though cast from lead, Pete Amaya slid through and was instantly lost from sight.

Uriah waited until Dobkins had closed the door, then turned toward the others. "Give him diversionary fire," he ordered. "Zeke, Lee, Joseph . . . the rest of you . . . go to the back door with Kant and open fire."

They were moving away in a body when a solitary shot burst the roadway's stillness. Then other shots sounded and Uriah called them back. "They've seen him. Get to the front windows instead. Give him cover fire. Remember now . . . aim at their gun flashes and aim low. Aim to kill!"

Lee crouched by the same window he'd shared moments before with Amaya. Someone shouldered down next to him; he did not look around to see who it was. Uriah's words dinned in his brain. He knew without looking around that the old warrior was standing, wide-legged and towering, in the center of the room. He could pinch his eyes closed and visualize the spray of spittle, the twisted face alight with strange intentness, with madness, while Uriah listened to some inner voice no one else could hear, and roared his orders, directing the joined battle.

"Aim low and mind now . . . no snap-shooting. Use your sights. Make every ball count . . . we don't have too many."

Lee forced himself to look out where unkind light from the sickle moon shone. He heard the ripped-out curse of the man beside him.

"There he goes. Oh, Lord, they forced him away from the buildings."

Pedro Amaya was out in the roadway running hard toward the south. It came sadly to Lee that he was fleeing the wrong way—away from them toward the open prairie beyond Union City. Then it stung him that the enemy fire had dwindled and died and for the space of a withheld breath he thought Amaya was going to make it, was going to fade into the darkness and escape.

Then a wisp of smoke spewed, and another, and another, with flat, powerful sounds behind them. More shots until the roadway reverberated with them and they fell without rhythm, slamming hard and deafening.

"Now!" Uriah screamed over the din. "Now! Give it to them!" He was watching the running shadow with wide-sprung eyes and contorted mouth.

The man beside Lee thrust his rifle past the bars and fired into a spigot of red-flash from a storefront across the way. At his second shot Lee saw a man spring up convulsively, half turn, and crumple. The noise was deafening and black-powder stench choked him, stung his eyes.

A hurtling cry from north of the jailhouse fluted as clear as a bell above the gunfire. There came a ragged reply from many throats and the rocketing thunder of approaching horses. Hope left the youngest Gorman in that instant. The soldier column had returned, or one of the big posses. Full realization came swiftly then. They were bottled up, surrounded. Nine desperate men against an army . . .

Uriah's loud groan came now. "He's shot! Oh, Lord, he's shot!"

Lee turned in time to see Pedro Amaya's distant small form wilt. In his heart he winced with each slug that tore the Mexican's flesh, twisting him, holding him suspended until more lead came to crash into his numbing body. Then Amaya was down. Flat down and unmoving with dust spurting around him.

Uriah's groan lingered, searingly clear in the boy's head. Never before in his lifetime had he heard his father give over to despair. Never once.

"Zeke! George! Come over here! Move fast now!"

Others twisted for a searching look at him, the despair in every face diluted by the most illogical hope. Uriah ignored everyone but his eldest son and George Dobkins. "We got to get out of here," he shot at them. "There's only one way left now, with Amaya gone. George, go fetch U'Ren. Zeke, get the Fosters. We'll bargain with 'em first."

"Paw, they won't bargain, dammit all."

"Get 'em anyway. We'll use 'em for shields then."

"Not the girl, Paw."

"Zeke, damn you . . . !"

Lee was moving across the room as he interrupted his father. "No! I've gone along, Paw, but here I quit."

"Quit!" Uriah roared. "Quit! You jellyfish you, there's not a man amongst us can quit now. You're fighting for your life now, boy. All of us are."

But Lee stood shoulder to shoulder with Zeke and in their eyes and faces Uriah read finality. Normally he would have broken them with his scorn, his mighty and towering contempt. Now there was not the time and he knew it. "All right," he said in a strangling way. "Leave the girl, then."

"And Lew, Paw."

Before Uriah could reply Kant U'Ren came up with George Dobkins. "The soldiers are filing in behind the jailhouse," he told him. "They got a mortar with 'em."

Uriah crooked his talon-like fingers at them and when they had all drawn close—all except Lew Foster sitting on a chair and Ann standing beside him watching—he started forward toward the door. Beyond, the gunfire was dying down.

"Make for the livery barn and get a horse. Don't stop if someone goes down. Don't even stop to give battle. There's no time for that now. Get astride and ride for it. Don't stop for anything. Ride west toward the mountains. Stay with the others as long as you can. We got strength so long as we stand together, but, if a horse goes down or gives out, don't turn back to help." The fingers closed around the drawbar; they grew white from straining. "I'm going to open this. As soon as I do, go. Run for it. Don't stop and don't look back and God go with you. This has been an honest fight and we've deserved success."

Lee watched the drawbar move. His mouth was dry and numb. He wasn't conscious of Ann saying his name. He wasn't even conscious of moving when Uriah yanked the drawbar clear with a report like a pistol shot and flung back the door, and the straining bodies around him impelled him forward out into the rattling gunfire and the sudden screaming turmoil of the roadway.

Lee ran swiftly with the others, northward toward the livery barn, only dimly conscious of the puffs of smoke and flashes of fire coming at them. He was aware of nothing, really, until a familiar pungency filled his head, its ammonia overtones clearing out the fumes and numbness. Ahead, Uriah's swinging form bobbed and weaved as he ran deeper into the livery barn. Behind him scurried Joseph Fawcett and Kant U'Ren side-by-side. Out of nowhere a blurred face appeared; it disappeared almost immediately in a burst of flame from George Dobkins's handgun.

"Horses!" Uriah was yelling. "Yonder in the tie stalls!"

They scattered toward the frightened animals that were rolling back their eyes and straining at their tie ropes. Lee glimpsed Zeke yank a rope loose, spin up on to a quivering back, and wheel the animal toward the barn's rear exit.

Uriah got astride, too, flinging himself against a plunging mount with scrabbling hands and flying beard, but never for a second loosening the hold on his rifle. Then the others were engulfed in orange lamplight, milling, cursing, mounting or falling back, and yelling for the others to wait, to help.

Lee had no trouble with the horse he found. It was a canny beast and old. Man-made panic did not readily penetrate its thick skull or easily disturb its small brain. It did not come to life until the rifle butt crashed against its side, then it plunged ahead with a snort.

Now the cowmen were rushing across the road. They were firing into the barn alleyway, adding to the din and confusion. Two men, one of them Zeke, swung and emptied pistols into the crowd and there was a burst of yells as the cowmen broke and fled. Next, Uriah's scream rose keening high and they followed him down the runway out into the paling night beyond. Behind, two sheepmen remained afoot. One had gotten astride but had been bucked off. They fought well but unwisely. Both fired at the same time and thus their guns came empty at the same time. They were shot to death as they cowered in a corner, and their bodies were shot into long after both were dead.

Doubled over targets on speeding horses in uncertain light made the worst possible targets, but they should all have been killed anyway if the number of bullets fired at them had counted, and once they were nearly stopped. A perceptive soldier ran his squad across their path, some hastily kneeling, the balance standing. But it was too late. Uriah's horse hit the officer first. He was knocked easily ten feet and lay broken in the curling dust. Other horses went over and through the squad. There were shots fired but they hit no one. The outlaws raced past and night closed after them.

Lee's horse proved swiftest of them all. He was overtaking his father when Uriah cried out and slammed his plunging beast back upon its haunches. Coming toward them in a blurred race was a great host of riders. The sheen of the sweat of their horses was visible. Lee leaned far over the side of his horse instinctively and shot past Uriah going westerly. The others followed his example and Uriah careened along beside Zeke, an ungainly figure squared into the light of a lowering moon, arms flopping and head thrust forward as though to aid his flight by sheer will alone.

The pursuit fought to stay within pistol range and for an hour it succeeded. Then the outlaws began steadily to draw away. Their horses were fresh. The other horses were not. Distant howls of frustration and rage came softly into the dawning day.

Lee's rifle was gone. He had no recollection of dropping it, nor did he speculate on it long. Instead he concentrated on the horse under him. Eventually, when he dared, he peered over his shoulder to watch the distance widen swiftly now between his companions and their pursuers. Then he laid low along the horse's neck and closed his eyes against the stinging lash of a whipping mane.

Around him the survivors were breaking out of the tight group a little. Uriah's shirt tail was whipping behind him and his thin long legs were wound around the horse beneath him like coiled springs. His shaggy hair flew and his beard was a speckled banner.

Off to one side Kant U'Ren rode low on his horse completely in rhythm with its movements, and behind him Zeke was thumping his mount with heels and rifle butt.

Joseph Fawcett had both fists wound into the mane of the animal he rode. He, too, had lost his rifle somewhere.

There were six of them left: Dobkins, U'Ren, Joseph Fawcett, Lee and Zeke Gorman, and Uriah. That was all. Bachelor and the others lay somewhere behind, either dead in the livery barn, killed before they got to it, or strung out on the prairie down their back trail. To Uriah their escape was a mighty victory. He counted them once, twice, looked back to be sure there were no more, then cried out to the survivors: "The Lord was with us, boys! Head for the uplands now and ride hard." In the same voice he added: "I think Fawcett's been hit."

Lee slowed after another mile to let the others come up. He had not heard his father speak of Fawcett, and, when Uriah flagged him onward, he turned dutifully and pushed on at a slower pace, leading them toward a bosque of cottonwoods that loomed up in the growing steel light of earliest dawn. There he stopped to blow his mount and to wait. When Uriah came up, he flung Lee his lead-rope rein and sprang down, walked swiftly back, and caught Joseph Fawcett as the latter began to slide earthward from his mount.

"We can't stay here long," Kant U'Ren said.

The others did not heed him. They were walking back where Uriah kneeled beside Fawcett.

When Lee moved restlessly, the half-breed said: "Here, give me the lines and go look, but tell 'em not to waste too much time."

There was a soft duskiness to the sky and a little fat star hung low above the horizon, easterly.

When Lee was approaching, he heard Uriah say: "He's hard hit, boys." He went closer, stopped, and stood transfixed, staring down at the gaping wound, uncovered and jelly-like where his father had skinned back Fawcett's sodden shirt. Then he kneeled across from Uriah and for just a moment an ill dizziness gripped him, then it passed. He reached out to staunch the rush of dark blood with a piece of rag someone pushed into his hand, wiped the blood away with long even strokes only to have it bubble upward again and pool below Joseph Fawcett's chest, in the sunken place of his belly.

"Clean through him . . . from behind," said Uriah, rocking back on his heels.

Lee felt Fawcett's eyes full on his face. He glared at his father. "Shut up, will you. Somebody find some water."

Uriah got up and shuffled off. The others followed him and Lee was left alone with the dying man.

Fawcett's lips were turning blue now. He no longer sought faces or the answer in other eyes to the consuming question in his head. Instead he pinched his eyes closed and struggled to breathe, and the boy kneeling in the new grass beside him knew what he was attempting was futile. Blood pushed through the rag, undiminished.

Thoughts screamed in the complete silence of Lee's brain: *You're dying, Fawcett. Paw's gone to hunt water, but it won't help. There's no use to suck air like that, Fawcett. We'll be here with you . . . this isn't going to take long. We'll bear the vigil with you. I'll stay, Fawcett. I'll stay. You're the fourth today I think, Fawcett. Pete was first. He didn't believe in anything. There'll be more. You were a brave man. You didn't have Paw's courage, his will and craftiness maybe, but you were a brave man because I know how scared you were in that jailhouse, waiting to be hung.*

"Kit . . ."

It was a soft whimper of sound and no other sound ever passed Joseph Fawcett's lips. *It's a name,* Lee thought. *Maybe you had a wife somewhere, or a daughter maybe. It doesn't matter now. You're brought low for no real reason, Fawcett. No particular reason, really. Not for range rights. I guess you've known this, too, for a few days now. I guess you've come to this like the rest of us will . . . because you were wound around Paw's finger. Blinded by his spell. Caught up and flung here like an autumn leaf. . . . Don't stare. Don't strain, Fawcett. Paw's gone for water. No, they didn't get us. We're clear, Fawcett. For maybe an hour we can stay here. In less than that you won't care any more. I know. I know, Fawcett . . . you're afire. You're burning up inside. It didn't smash your soft parts. It went clean through your backbone and out your lungs. I can hear them filling up. I got no idea what's inside you, but I can hear the sloshing every time you breathe.*

Joseph Fawcett's eyes bulged with dimming sight. His lips fell open and a whining chant began. A toneless thing that rose and fell, bubbled and frothed, and grew finally still, only to come again weaker, an eerie ageless whimper that went down deep into the listener, found response in dark places of his spirit, and drew out a thin, dim memory of primitive things eons distant. Then it stopped altogether and the whispering dawn turned soft with a soughing wind dragging through the cottonwoods and Joseph Fawcett's head began to rock feebly from side to side, eyes clamped closed tightly.

Uriah returned noiselessly, stood over them a

moment, then kneeled down. He had a hatful of spring water. Lee took it, cradled the dying man's head in his arm, and poured water across his face. Fawcett gulped, choked, and swallowed avidly. Continued to swallow after the hat was emptied, its last brown dregs gone, until Lee laid him back. He heard a roaring the others could not hear. There was a dimming to his mind. He tried to speak again. Only an unintelligible husking sound came. His mouth sagged and Joseph Fawcett was dead.

Lee bent low to search for the heartbeat that was not there. He straightened up, looked long at the filthy, haggard face. It grew soft, mellow with a beauty, a peacefulness it had never possessed in life. And the body flattened, widened, caved in gently. A finger of quiet wind ruffled Fawcett's black hair and moved on.

"He's dead."

"Yes," Uriah acknowledged. "And for the peace it brings I could near trade places with him."

"He didn't die peaceful, Paw. He died hard."

Uriah got up. The unreasoning quick wrath was on him and breath whistled past his nostrils. "Don't contradict me, boy."

"No, I won't, Paw. Not here. Not if it defiles this spot where Fawcett died."

"Nor mock me either, damn you!"

A redness swam before Lee's eyes and impaired his vision. He was mute.

"Between you and me there's been little enough lately, boy," said Uriah. "If you got hate in you like some of the others have . . ."

"I've got no hatred, Paw. It's defeat I got in me, not hatred."

"Then," Uriah retorted swiftly, "you're the first of our blood to have it, I'll covenant you that."

"Maw didn't?"

Uriah's fists knotted. He stood oaken and raw-boned and towering forbiddenly above dead Joseph Fawcett. "The fever taken your maw off and you know it."

"I don't believe that," Lee answered, facing half away from Uriah. "I don't believe that and I don't think you do. She'd been too many years fighting against . . . everything. It wasn't the fever, Paw, it was despair. It was defeat. Fighting every living hour against something she couldn't hope to win out over."

"What? I ask you what couldn't be won out over, boy?"

"You, mostly. You and conditions, I guess. About the other things I don't know. About you . . . I *do* know. I don't understand, but I know it was mostly you, Paw. Maw couldn't win out over you and neither can I. Neither can the rest of us."

Lee cast a long final sorrowing look at the still body and peaceful gray face between them against dawn's cooling earth, then he walked swiftly toward the trees where the others were sitting like scarecrows, faces turned away and wearing inward expressions.

Uriah followed him with his green eyes until he was lost in the rising mists. Then he turned a slower look upon fallen Joseph Fawcett, and his face turned darkly brooding. *I will not give up,* he thought. *I have never given up. It is not in me to do so . . . but, God, I'm tired and they hate me. All of them now, even Ezekiel. They follow now because there is nothing left. They fight like cornered rats now, not like men fighting for their rights. Where did I go wrong?*

We are fighting for our rights, for equal graze on open range. That is right. We have right on our side. No. No, not any more. Somewhere something went wrong. We are outlawed. Something has happened. I, too, am an outlaw now. Am I responsible?

I think not, by God. I think not at all. I think what has gone wrong is the same thing that has been wrong all along. We are sheepmen and they are cowmen and the law is cowman law. That's what is wrong. Not I. I have done no more than lead them against injustice. As God is my witness, I will lead them still. I am right! And I will triumph. This will not end as Appomattox did. It will not end as things ended in Alabama and Tennessee . . . as things have always ended. I feel it in me . . . this time I will win out. I've got to. I must. Because there will never be another chance to triumph over wrong . . . not for me at my age. And I leave no flesh of my flesh to fight on after me. Not in Ezekiel . . . certainly not in Lee.

Then, Jesus, I pray to You for strength . . . for guidance. . . .

He felt a burning in his eyes, a wetness. "Good night, Fawcett. You fought well . . . a good fight. I will remember you. Now good night. We've got to be riding."

He turned away, strode toward the others, still and drooping low among the cottonwood trees. In the east a pink stain of approaching day appeared. The trees and men and played-out horses rose sharply against the sky's paleness.

Chapter Thirteen

Lee stood briefly among the trees where the horses were, then he took them by the lead ropes and went out where new grass was thick and succulent so they could replenish their energy. He squatted among them with the pleasant sound of their eating drawing away the tension. He saw his father come toward the others, speak curtly, and watched them all return to the spot where Fawcett was cooling out. Then came the soft thud of rocks being dropped, first against flesh, later against other rocks, until the cairn was finished. He could picture the gaunt frame kneeling, arranging rocks, fitting them, forcing them into place.

How many gone now? Percy Bachelor had fled; they had not had him at the jailhouse so he had made good his escape. Baker and one other back at the livery barn. Fawcett . . . Paxton Clement, Manuel Cardoza, Slocum, Hoag, Logan, Amaya, Pompa . . . Others. It seemed a long time ago. Dead for what? Because his father's answer for everything these fast-falling years had been an upraised fist, a harsh word, a roar of defiance.

They were returning now, boots swishing through the grass, silent filthy scarecrows who even took their guns with them to graveside.

He continued to squat in apathy among the horses, listening to the tiny voice of memory. He felt hunger, but not only the hunger for food. Somewhere along the back trail he'd lost something out of himself. Something that had always been strong and bright and confident within him. Something that had been inherent right up until last night. Now it was forever gone; he would not find it again. It was youth.

He'd lost youth. Somewhere, very recently, he'd forgotten how to smile, to laugh, to see beauty in ugliness, had forgotten what confidence was. It was difficult now to see high color and dancing light and no longer could his outstretched hand encounter warmth and promise in all he touched.

One of the horses threw up its head. For a moment the alarm did not break over the man. Then it did, fully. The horse was not looking easterly where the others were returning from Fawcett's rock cairn, it was straining due south.

A steel fingernail scraped along Lee's spine. He spun up off the ground. A second animal raised its head, then a third and fourth.

"Paw!"

The plodding figures froze, then they rushed forward, their apathy gone in a twinkling. Uriah's brooding expression evaporated in that instant. Without searching the brightening skyline, he hissed: "Bring those horses back into the trees."

Lee obeyed with rough swiftness. Zeke ran to help. Like the others, he was swift and sure now, in every movement. "Here, give me a couple of those ropes."

Among the trees four tense shadows waited in watchful suspense, guns at the ready. When the brothers hastened up, Kant U'Ren was sniffing, his head up high and working back and forth.

Uriah grabbed his mount, twisted up a squaw bridle, and jerked it tight. "What was it, boy?" he demanded of Lee.

"I don't know. Something, though. The horses heard it or smelled it . . . south of us there."

"Maybe wolves or coyotes."

Uriah snorted and turned a cold look on the man who had said that—George Dobkins. "These're range bred horses, boy. They're not about to get in any sweat over coyotes or wolves."

Kant U'Ren saw no sense in this talk. "We been

here too long already," he growled. "Let's get going."

Uriah was already swinging astride. He settled himself squarely, then watched the others. Only five now.

"Head west for the first ridge. We can see from up there. Follow me."

Zeke was ready to spring up when his horse flung up its head with flaring nostrils. Quick as a flash big Zeke's steel fingers clamped down hard, cutting off his wind. They did not slacken until the beast was struggling for air.

"Nicker will you? Damn you, be quiet!"

They rode northerly behind Uriah, staying to the trees as long as possible. Then out into the graying light and across open prairie until the country sucked back and dipped slightly before it began to buckle up and rise steadily into the mountains beyond.

They were all uneasy but Kant U'Ren seemed most disturbed. To Lee he growled: "Wasted a half hour back there, god dammit. It's sunup now. We should've been into the hills long ago."

Lee was mute. He did not care.

"Folks'll be boiling out of their settlement like bees out of a hive."

"Let them," the boy answered. "Kant, how long do you think this can last?"

U'Ren's gaze came back, lingered in stony silence on Lee a moment, then drifted away, went forward where Uriah rode out ahead a short distance, and remained there.

"Your Paw's a fox, boy. He brought us out of Union City. Don't forget that."

"Yes. He brought us out of Union City. Look around you, Kant. How many do you see who rode *into* Union City with us?"

The half-breed would have answered that but Lee didn't wait. He urged his horse forward, up where Zeke rode just behind their father. They exchanged looks, nods, but no words. What was there to talk of? They were hungry, yes, but they'd always been more or less hungry. They were hunted. Their chances were momentarily lessening. Once they could race over the prairie, even easterly, beyond the cowmen's town. Now they could go only toward the mountains. The land behind was locked against them. Even the mountains were watched but at least they knew them, knew where they might lie down and go soft against the earth for a while. But in the end it would be the same—spring up and flee, ride for it.

They hadn't even saddles now and some were without rifles. They dared not make even a dry-oak fire. Sharp noses would detect it.

And all the time the ring was tightening.

What was there to talk about? Winning a range war they'd lost first in Paxton Clement's ranch yard—and last night amid the dead and dying back at Union City—or before that, during the cold-blooded murder of Captain Gower Hardin?

There was nothing to say. Nothing at all. They were done with words and shortly they would also be done with deeds. The land was swarming against them; it rang with the promise of quick hard justice. Men talked of the future—they had none. They talked of the past—they had no wish to remember. Of the present? No, there was no present, really. There were only moments and any of them might be their last. They rode together through the warming daylight following the eldest Gorman, totally silent, with faces averted, with tired eyes, troubled and tortured and watchful. Around them was an army of vengeful, hard-riding men in a closing circle. It could only be a matter of time.

Uriah led them to a thin, long ridge, and halted to look back.

They had to be very careful now, since behind them were the rooting posses and ahead, probably on the high places, were cowboy sentinels waiting to catch movement. Elsewhere there was thin rising mist and fading shadows. A rim of strong light was descending the mountain sides behind them, blood-red near the peaks and pink below where gloom diluted it.

Zeke sat his horse between his father and his brother. He was looking steadily downward across the empty world. He was relaxed and slouched. "For now we'd best stand fast right here," he told them. "They'll be watching for movement." From the corner of his eye Zeke saw his father draw up stiffly. "I know," he added quickly. "You're captain here. I was thinking out loud."

Coldness drew out across his father's face. "That's right. I'm captain here. You remember that, boy."

The others stirred. They were embarrassed for Zeke. They knew Uriah was thinking back to the fight at the knoll.

"I've had experience at this sort of thing. Don't any of you forget that. I do what's best for us."

In Lee an unusual flash of fierce anger rose up at his father's words. It was bitter anger. It would be hard to convince Fawcett that Uriah always did what was best for them. And Pompa, Bachelor, Cardoza, Amaya . . . The hand on his rope rein quaked in tightening spasms. Then Uriah spoke a hard truth that winnowed away Lee's sudden wrath, leaving him drained and spent.

"But even if I didn't . . . even if what we are doing is wrong . . . it wouldn't matter because now we are all of a feather. If they take us alive, we're slated to die on their scaffolding. If they catch us on the prairie, they'll shoot us down like dogs. We must stay together and fight together."

Yes, thought the youngest son. *And die together.*

They followed Uriah deeper into the hills, twisting and turning through horse-high brush, their bodies bumped and bruised and scratched but hidden at least. Moving cautiously through the dark cañons toward a secret place Uriah knew, and finally they could stop in a tree-roofed tiny glade and get down, turn out the horses, and drink deeply at a seepage spring where the punky earth was covered with hair-fine grass and moss. The softest bed they had known in weeks.

Later, when the others went out a ways to find places of concealment where they might rest, Lee remained by the spring alone, listening until the last man-made sounds were no more. Then he lay back and for the first time in days felt completely alone and detached. His mind, despite danger, went down the years with a poignancy he could not fathom. Days faded into nights, then grew light again; time growing into years spinning out lazily, heavy and solid with memory. Times he and Zeke had gone pokeberry gathering for their mother. Days working the vats making lye soap, mulching oak ashes into the cauldrons. A richness of familiarity blossoming between them with their mutual understanding and silence, and always somewhere close had been the old man's shadow, hulking large.

Other faces faded and glowed shadow-like but always somewhere nearby in the processes of memory stood Zeke—and their father, oaken and gnarled and brooding silently, fierce and seeming mighty.

The old horse he had stolen cat-footed up to the

spring, eyed him askance, and drank. The specters from yesteryear dissolved and there was just this stolen horse beside him and pervading silence throbbing in the dulling shade and the summer warmth, with peaceful little rustling sounds in the grass and the gold-blue sky overhead. He smelled horse sweat and summer heat. . . .

Where once there had been fourteen of them there were now only five. Somewhere out on the range near a bosque of cottonwoods was Fawcett's cairn.

Farther back, even, was Ann. Haunted eyes, a still, impassive face in memory standing fully upright and gazing steadily into his face with her two souls in one body.

He fell asleep with warming sunlight filtering through tree leaves, etching soft patterns of gold across him. Ten feet away his stolen horse drowsed, too. It was peaceful there. Too peaceful.

He had no idea how long he had slept, or even, upon awakening, exactly where he was. All he knew was that gunshots were ringing through the pinched-down little arroyo and many men were screaming. There came, too, a clatter of riders. He whirled up off the ground like a startled hawk. Whoever it was came in force. He reached the equally as surprised horse in two bounds and sprang upon its back and spun westerly, still befogged by sleep. *No, not westerly*—instinct told him—*that's the direction the horsemen are approaching.* He saw three riders squirt past and lose themselves up the cañon, riding low and faces white. He would have followed them but the horse shied from a near hit that sliced a white sliver of living wood off a tree, and lit facing easterly. He bent low and slammed inward with his heels. The beast needed no urging, only directing. It fled in panic through filigreed shadows, its rider shivering with dread and choking fear.

He let the horse have its head, keeping it only in this easterly direction that seemed open to it. Man-high brush did the rest, shielding them both except for blurred glimpses where they broke into openings, crossed them, and plunged deeper into shadows.

He topped out over the same ridge they had sat upon that morning, then plunged down the far side with thoughtless abandon. Ahead the country was open as far as the cottonwood bosque. Down across the running dip of land and toward the only cover within miles—where Joseph Fawcett lay.

He reached it safely and drew up to blow the horse. The respite proved too brief. Suddenly from behind came the strong-throated yell of pursuit and his heart darkened with fear again. He leaned low and the horse shot forward, belly-down and with little ears flattened. He rode with trees hurtling past, heading north, with matted shadows to screen him. After a time hope revived when he could not hear them behind him any longer, and later, with dusk curdling, with the shadows intensifying, he left the trees, loped across open country, and did not draw up until he'd passed several ranches. Once, a great slavering hound paced him with lolling tongue, baying in a booming way until Lee reined southerly and lost him with a burst of speed.

He knew instinctively that he was not far distant from Union City's northerly environs, but with night falling now he could not exactly place where he was. It did not matter. All that mattered was that he kept clear of others and kept moving.

Where several log houses clustered close he went furtively afoot, leading the horse for extra silence. Clear of them he thudded over the endless range with a glow of star shine over his right shoulder. Far back, looming blacker than night, were the mountains; he kept them in position to set a course by.

The world had never seemed so foreign a place to him as it did this night. The stars lacked warmth; they were too high and small for kinship, and when the moon finally rose it was curled inward in a sick way. Only the old horse beneath him was friendly.

Then, believing himself well east of Union City, he quartered southerly meaning to ride until he dropped, and then ride some more until Wyoming was far behind him.

He stopped several times, put his ear to the

earth, and held his breath. The last time, he heard the beating of a solitary rider coming toward him from the west. He waited to hear others, too, but there was only that solitary pounding. A lone rider might mean anything or nothing. It might even mean Uriah or Zeke had escaped the attack, also. It might be just a traveler, or a messenger carrying tidings to Union City.

For a time he sat like stone, waiting to hear the sound from horseback. Then restlessness seized him. Each second was precious. The horse fidgeted impatiently and he studied the flat dark world. He did not know which way to go. Finally he rode deep into a sage patch, dismounted, and squatted there, looking out, letting the moon gather strength to brighten the night. Eventually he saw pale ribbons of a roadway and concluded it must be the northern passage to Union City. The rider he had detected was probably riding it somewhere although he could not see him or hear him now. Perhaps he had passed by. Fear returned. If that was so, if the man had gone on southerly and was a messenger, he could rouse the cowmen athwart Lee's withdrawal route, and at any dip or rise of the prairie he would meet a band of enemies.

His fear was feeding upon itself, consuming him and contorting his thoughts. He had no inkling that he, like the others, was helpless and lost without Uriah. He got back onto the horse and sat there, motionless as an Indian, heeding the fear with his rope rein hanging, his mind aching, his body racked with the pain of stress, and his belly as empty as a wet sack. The sound of drowsy birds in the sage scolding him sounded as loud as pistol shots.

Then a slow-growing clatter of horsemen came whisper soft from up the road, north, and he spun the horse, forcing it deeper into the brush. He sprang down again and laid a big hand across the beast's nostrils. His heart was thudding. The sound grew stronger, went echoing down the roadway and out through the night with a rhythmic pounding insistence.

Soldiers! They came into ghostly view, a long line of them riding in twos with a whipping bird-tailed pennant out ahead. He was not mistaken. No other body of men rode with that swinging sound, with that clash of metal scabbards, and that peculiar cadence.

The fear returned overpoweringly. He cringed and his courage fled. There was no escape now to the south, in the direction the soldiers were taking. The way was blocked westerly toward the mountains. Northerly were the big ranches and easterly it was the same. Men were everywhere riding to the kill. The certainty of all this pressed in, making him light-headed. Even if any of them could escape, they would never cease to be hunted. There would be rewards, bounty hunters, eager guns everywhere seeking to snuff out his life. The full knowledge that this was immutably so cowed him.

Beyond, the soldiers were swinging past in their long dark line. There were no words among them, no signs, just the rise and fall of men on big horses whose faces were hidden by hat-shadowing darkness and whose hands were skeletal in bone-white gauntlets. A winking of curved saber scabbards.

He let out an unconscious cry, dug into the old horse cruelly, and burst out of the brush in a crazy run toward the roadway where dust curled lazily upward and hung poised in the stillness of night. He reined up sharply near the end of the column and threw up his arms.

"Soldiers . . . soldiers! Hold up! Wait!"

Their startled faces turned toward him. Puddled eyes stared out of deep shadows.

"Hold up!"

A voice came thinly over the clatter, others took it up, tossed it the length of the column, and finally the riders slowed, milled, and halted.

"What is it . . . back there?"

"Settler, sir. Hollered for us to halt."

Lee's arms dropped. In the heavy silence he watched a thin, sparse man ride toward him down the side of the column. A monstrous upcurling mustache made the man's face look fierce. He saw suspicion in the eyes and mercilessness in the tightly puckered mouth.

"Who are you? What do you want, sir?"

"I want to give up, mister. I'm Lee Gorman."

The officer drew up and sat still, gazing steadily ahead at the bareback scarecrow. He saw no weapons, which made his face cloud with doubt. "Is that so," he said flatly. "You're Lee Gorman, are you?"

"Yes, sir."

"Where is your father?"

"I don't know, sir."

"Don't know?"

"No, sir. We split up. I don't know where he is. Or Zeke. Or the others."

"Are you lying to me?"

"No, sir."

"Why did you split up?"

"We were jumped back in the mountains. I ran for it. So did the others. I don't know where they went. I came down here . . . I got lost."

Stony silence. The soldiers were straining to hear. Lee was conscious of their blurred faces in the weak light.

"You might be telling the truth. God knows you look like you are."

"I am, sir."

"But you must know what your father's plans were."

"He had none. We did what he told us. He said life was how you found it. We didn't know from hour to hour where he would take us."

The merciless cold face was without expression or movement. "I see. And how many of you are left?"

"There were five of us left."

"It was reported that at least six of you escaped Union City last night."

"One died. Joseph Fawcett died, sir. He was shot through. He is buried under some rocks not far from Cottonwood Creek."

"Good. That is one less." The officer turned only his head. "Corporal! Four-man escort for the prisoner!"

He rode back toward the head of the column without another glance, and a large gloved hand closed over Lee's arm.

"In here, Gorman. There. Now don't try to break out."

"I won't. I surrender, sir."

The corporal was heavy-faced, solid and square in a shapeless but massively powerful way. He gazed steadily at Lee, then cleared his throat, spat, and held out some rock-hard biscuits.

"Here, boy. You might as well eat some, too. Because of your old man we been riding near sixty miles on nothing else."

Chapter Fourteen

The column with Lee in its midst rode steadily for nearly an hour, neither slackening its pace nor stopping until it clattered into Union City where a few late lamps burned, casting enormously grotesque shadows behind where the ranks were wheeled into line and halted.

There were a few men abroad, mostly sentinels with rifles told off to this duty by cow interests. They listened to the curt order that dismounted the soldiers and watched the tall, thin officer go down the line, plucking off his gauntlets. His orders were precise and impersonal; he was a man with a duty to perform. Nothing more and nothing less. The cowmen watched him from unfriendly faces, dour-looking and silent. It was their historic plaint that soldiers never arrived until the fighting was over. They were clearly thinking this now.

Then one of them saw the prisoner and moved closer for a better look. He drew up erect and yelled in full throat: "They got one! They got the youngest Gorman!"

There was a stir among those sparse spectators. Men moved closer, peering hard, then they, too, took up the cry. It echoed back and forth, filling the roadway until Union City rang with it. Men tumbled from saloons and houses. They filled the plank walks and the roadway. The thin officer watched this tumultuous eruption briefly, then he said: "Sergeant! Close up the ranks! Corporal! Detail horse holders and reinforce the prisoner guard!"

Townsmen swarmed. They cried out for young Gorman, punctuating each demand with fierce profanity.

The officer straightened his back against them. "Sabers!" he called out. "The flat of your sabers, men . . . no shooting." He faced the largest mob of civilians, and although he raised his voice, it was still dispassionate-sounding. "Stay back!"

A squat man, thick-thewed as a spruce tree stopped close to Lee's guard detail. His legs were planted widely and he seemed silently undecided. Others bumped him, jostled him, but he scarcely moved. Yells burst over his head. Still he remained silent.

"There he is . . . in there!"

"Drag the murderer out. Take him to the gibbet."

"Come on, boys, they won't use them swords."

Close to Lee the corporal said: "Steady. Steady now. No running through. . . . Here, you damned scum . . . back off or I'll lay your skull open. Back now, damn you. . . ."

The soldiers tightened their circle. Lee could see their white faces, could feel the quiver of their tightly strung bodies, and beyond them was a surging sea of wrathful faces. Huge words stood starkly in his mind. *They want to lynch me. This is crazy. They're going to attack the soldiers.*

Then the squat man roared: "Stop! Leave off that shoving. Settle down a minute. They got him."

"Yes," swore a young blond giant, waving a Dragoon pistol. "They got him and we aim to take him."

Others supported the big youth with their cries.

"He'll get his . . . wait and see if he don't!"

"There'll be a trial!" cried the squat man.

"Trial, hell! He'll hang right now . . . tonight. Damned if he won't. No bluebellies going to keep us from it."

"Hey, blacksmith, you gone yellow? Get outta the way then, an' let some men handle this!"

"Quit that kind of talk," the squat man said, turning toward the mob. "Dammit, shut up, will you?"

The blond giant muscled closer to the squat man. Lee could plainly see his face. It was round and flat and splotchy with excited dark blood. "Shut up yourself, blacksmith!" he bellowed. "Who'n hell you think you are anyway? You and your yellow talk." From within the circle Lee watched them. The squat man faced fully toward the huge youth, whose corn-silk hair was awry and tumbling and who still waved his big pistol. He thought they would fight, and, thought if they did, the madness would erupt and would fill the roadway with terrible violence.

"Been eleven of us killed by them god-damned sheepmen!"

The wild anger beat upon the night air. Fisted hands shook and weapons waved aloft.

The officer apparently thought as Lee did, for he opened a way toward the bristling opponents with his saber. Its burning glow went past the squat man and stopped only inches from the giant's belly. "Get back and shut up," said the officer, leaning slightly forward so that his saber tip lay against the youth's shirt. "I mean that. Get back or I'll gut rip you!"

The youth sucked back and looked up the saber's curved length of bright steel. "Put it down and I'll thrash you till you beg."

The officer's impersonal coldness was both a contrast and a significant thing. He meant what he said and those around him knew it.

The squat man moved away from him toward the youth. He reached for the boy's belt. "Don't force him, lad. Come on, forget it."

"No, by Lord A'mighty, I'll kill 'em both!"

The officer moved his wrist. The youth's mouth snapped closed and a pinpoint of blood appeared on his shirt.

"I'll run you through!"

The squat man had the youth's belt now. He gave a powerful tug and drew the boy away.

That was the high point of the night. Afterward the crowd drew back a little. Its roar diminished and its eyes followed the thin officer as he moved back a little, saber still gripped hard but down now. And when next he spoke in that expressionless voice, he had won his victory.

"Draw pistols! Ready! Aim . . ."

There remained but one word to say. He did not say it but the crowd knew that he would. They gave way, those in front pushing toward the rear, their defiant clamorings turned now to quick demands for passage through.

Lee felt the burly corporal's body go loose beside him. He heard the belly-deep sigh. Then the officer was speaking again.

"Corporal! Your detail is detached. Take the prisoner to the jailhouse, lock him up, and post sentinels with orders to shoot."

"Yes, sir!"

They led him away, four soiled soldiers with resolute faces and hating eyes. Behind them were the blue ranks ready to fire upon any who interfered with them. None did. The crowd was melting away. It watched Lee pass in hard silence.

Then, back a ways, the officer's unmistakable voice said: "Sergeant! Detach a squad. Arrest that big blond man and jail him." Over the sound of booted feet grinding through the roadway's dust in cadence, the same voice continued to speak. "The rest of you . . . listen. This town is under martial law. There will be no public assembly . . . overt acts against soldiers will be considered rebellion

. . . under the Articles of War I am entitled to enforce the law. I am also entitled to use firing squads to do it. I will use them. Now disperse . . . go to your homes, do not assemble, and stay quiet."

At the jailhouse Lee turned for a glimpse backward. The men were moving off, splintering off in ones and twos, and pacing homeward through the night. The corporal pushed him roughly. "Go on, boy." He stumbled into the lighted office with its empty gun rack and halted.

There were two men with badges inside. Lee recognized neither of them. They wore impassive looks and ignored him in favor of the corporal. In spite of himself he sought the chair where Lew Foster had sat, and the spot beside it where Ann had stood.

"Lock him up," said the corporal, and after this had been done, he held out his hand for the keys. The deputies did not comply immediately. "Listen, boys," the burly soldier said complainingly, "Union City's under martial law. Maybe you were the law, but you ain't now. Gimme those keys." He got them. "Thanks. Now get out of here."

"Wait a minute, soldier. Just . . ."

"You want me to write it for you? Union City is under martial law. You understand what that means?"

"Well . . . ?"

"Then I'll tell you. Civil law . . . which is you . . . is suspended. The Army's running your town. You got no authority. Keep your badges and your guns . . . just walk out of here quiet-like. Don't make no fuss, boys, or I'll throw your god-damned butts in jail. Get out of here!"

The corporal's voice had been steadily rising. His last four words were loudly snarled. The deputies left, and the corporal looked around the room. His men were leaning along the wall; they were dog-tired and uncomfortable.

"Must be a coffee pot around here some place," said the corporal. "See can we find it, boys."

The men were moving off when their officer appeared in the doorway. Behind him lurked a shapely shadow.

"Corporal!"

"Sir?"

"This lady has my permission to see the prisoner."

"Yes, sir!"

This was a surprising thing. Old Ice-Water-For-Blood lived by the book. Why was he allowing a civilian to see the prisoner—and of all things a girl? He watched her come into the room. She was big-busted and handsome. The corporal's temples beat with hot blood. Her face was expressionless, her eyes steady and troubled. She was the stuff from which the strong common life came. He had not seen such a woman in weeks.

"Corporal!"

"Yes, sir!"

He led her past the gawking men and rattled the keys at Lee's door. Beyond the strap steel his prisoner looked outward with burning intensity.

"Ann!" The name went past his lips with forced breath.

The corporal got the door open and stood back to let her pass. Then he closed the door, locked it, and said: "Call when you want out, ma'am."

They waited until he was gone, then she faced him. "What happened, Lee?"

He told her while moving toward a straw pallet. She followed him at first only with her eyes, but, when he sank down, she went over and kneeled by him, listening and seeing how gaunt and old he had become.

"Did they get your father?"

"No . . . I don't know. We parted and I don't know what happened to Paw or Zeke or the others."

"Are you hurt, Lee?"

"No. Just worn out I guess. Tired plumb through." He closed his eyes and tossed gently on the pallet.

"Lie still." She fell silent. He felt her cool, gentle hands moving over him slowly, healingly. He wanted terribly to sleep, to let her hands draw away the tension so that he could turn all loose and soft, but there was a nagging in his head.

"Fawcett's dead and buried, Ann."

"All right, Lee. Rest quiet now."

"What happened to you . . . to your paw?"

"Nothing. After you got away, they came to the jailhouse and cut Paw loose."

"I want to remember something, Ann."

"Never mind. It's all over now, I think." Her hands grew still upon his chest. Lay there without pressure.

"Sleep, Lee."

"No. I remember what it was. You. When they caught us together and you fainted one of them said you were with child. He said he had five daughters and he knew it for a fact." His eyes sprang wide open.

"Are you, Ann?"

"Yes."

He would have started up but her palms pressed against him. She was not looking at his face.

"Lee, you've got to rest quiet."

There was something besides tiredness in her expression—something that had leached away the bloom—something dull and hopeless.

"Listen, Ann . . ."

"Lee, they're going to hang you."

Reaction came slowly, but finally he blinked and swallowed and lay back. Then, his body let go, turned all loose, and sagged down upon the pallet.

"I guess they will. I guess I'm plumb beat, Ann. I guess for us it's hopeless . . . isn't it?"

Her hands began to move again, working the great cords of his chest. "Just lie quiet and rest," she said. "It's all over now."

He did not speak again and a rattling sigh went out of him. Yes, it was all over. The running, the killing, the hunger, the grating of sleepless eyes in sand-lined sockets, the sour smell of dirty bodies, the everlasting fear. It was all over. There remained but one more thing to be done, and that didn't take long. Maybe a minute—maybe a few seconds.

Paw had said often the bullet hadn't yet been molded nor the man made who could best a Gorman. Well, he was wrong. It wasn't going to be a bullet or a solitary man. It was going to be hundreds of men and a hemp rope.

They were finally bested, every single one of them. But most of all the dead ones—the Pompas and Fawcetts and Amayas, and for all he knew the others, too. Maybe even the old man himself was dead.

He fell asleep, deeply asleep, and the hours passed. Ann left. The fragrance of coffee overrode other smells in the jailhouse. Dawn came. The sun rose high and golden warmth returned. He slept on.

Town Marshal Bob Ander and Deputy U.S. Marshal Burt Garner rode into Union City shortly after 9:00 a.m. They heard the news of Lee's capture while he slept. They went together to stand outside his cage and look in. Then they left together, seeking food and rest.

Others visited the jailhouse, mostly out of curiosity, until orders came for the corporal to admit only civilian law officers or military personnel. He was glad to comply because each intrusion interrupted his napping.

Union City was quiet. It was surly and it was unfriendly but it was quiet. Men sat in the saloons, drinking and looking into space. Posses were still out but generally they had been replaced by troops.

Now came the waiting.

The sheepmen were crushed, true, but Uriah Gorman had not been found. They wanted him above all others.

Soldiers hunted in droves. They sought him among the westering wagons of emigrants by the light of the moon with pitch-pine knots held high while they rummaged through the duffle of strangers. Poked and pried every place a man might hide. They even sent details far back into the forgotten cañons because some thought Indians might be hiding him.

Of the others there was only this word. A man answering the description of one George Dobkins had been found at the glade, dead. Shot, yes, but his death was more directly attributable to the fact that his horse had fallen on him. His skull was crushed to fragments.

Lee learned this in time from the corporal and from Ann, who had permission to visit him every day. But like the others, Lee had no tidings of his father or brother, or even of Kant U'Ren.

The land seethed with rumors. Each breath of air brought new ones. Uriah had been seen down in Arizona—he had robbed a bank in Texas—he was with renegades in Indian Territory—he'd been seen upon a flinty ridge not far from Bethel with the moon flowing full behind him, a gray and gaunt old wolf of a man holding high his rifle in a gnarled fist. And again, he was marauding with hostile red men spreading terror and desolation across the far frontier, beard flying, green eyes wild with madness, fading into the night in the lead of a silent, fierce army of warriors.

The summer days droned on and by early August it began to be accepted that Uriah Gorman had escaped. There began a low growl demanding that Lee be tried. He at least should be made to pay. In reply to each civilian demand the mustached officer made the identical reply.

"When the evidence is ready his trial will be held. It will be an orderly trial and until it is held you people will stay away from the jailhouse."

They stayed away. The officer had eleven of them in jail now. He ruled with an iron hand and an eye as cold as new steel. They did not like him in Union City. They did not like him at all but they certainly respected him.

Deputy U.S. Marshal Garner and Town Marshal Bob Ander talked to Lee for hours. They had everything he said transcribed. They were not unkind to him, and in the end, just before it was announced that his trial would begin, they seemed to be in silent sympathy. The fact was that they had both, over coffee and whiskey, come to the same conclusion: Lee was not a fighter; he had followed Uriah because he had not had the guts to break away and because he did not want to leave his brother. But he had followed him.

They accompanied Lee to the place of his trial. It was out of doors amid a precise square stepped off by blue ranks with the hot dust of summer in his nostrils and the high-riding sun above. There were too many witnesses for it to be held in any building of Union City, and in fact the officer wished it to be public anyway. Beyond his firm blue lines were townsmen, cowmen, and strangers. The free-graze war had raged better than three months; there were newsmen from such distant places as Sacramento down in California, Independence, Missouri, and even one elegant dude smelling splendidly of French toilet water from New York. They were indignant, these newsmen, because they were accorded no recognition by Captain Ice-Water-For-Blood and had to remain outside the blue cordon with the common herd.

Lee had to stand. He was manacled and wore an Oregon Boot—a steel leg fetter. The officer was seated behind a scarred saloon table. His pistol and sword lay in front of him, along with a sheaf of papers. He regarded the prisoner impassively, looked around at the two non-commissioned clerks who sat ready, pens poised and waiting, then he rapped with his fist for silence.

Beyond the ranks civilians gaped, jostled one another, and the eddying wash of their buzzing dwindled.

"This martial court is now in session for the purpose of hearing all evidence for and against the prisoner before this bar . . . Robert Edward Lee Gorman.

"Presiding officer is Captain Lemuel Spannaus, Fourth United States Cavalry. Officer for the defense is Lieutenant Gordon Meade, Fourth United States Cavalry. For the prosecution is Lieutenant Harold J. Bertram, Fourth United States Cavalry. . . ."

Another sharp rap.

"This martial court is now in session. Anyone causing a disturbance or in any way attempting to abrogate the dignity, interfere with the processes, or color the judgment herewith, shall be arrested and tried according to any pertinent Army Regulations and Articles of War.

"Lieutenant Bertram will read the bill of particulars. Lieutenant . . ."

The stillness deepened. By looking slightly to his left Lee could see Ann sitting on a bench among the witnesses. She was listening to the lieutenant's droning voice, as was everyone else, but her gaze was fully on his face. She was very pale.

Beside her sat her father. He was listening with his head lowered, gazing earthward. His shoulders were slumped forward. Flanking him was Paxton Clement's haggard wife and her two children. There were others, at least two dozen of them, but these four would have direct testimony to give and it was very clear that before this officer only that kind of testimony would suffice.

Lieutenant Bertram finished reading. Full silence descended. The golden sun beat down. Ander and U.S. Deputy Marshal Garner sat slightly apart with riot guns across their knees. They were looking straight at the officer.

"Robert Edward Lee Gorman, you have heard the charges against you. How do you plead . . . guilty or innocent?"

"Guilty, sir."

"Guilty of what? Of all the charges?"

"Uh . . . just guilty, sir."

The captain's cold eyes moved only slightly. "Lieutenant Meade."

"Yes, sir?"

"Have you consulted with the prisoner?"

"Yes, sir. But he wasn't communicative, sir. He told me only that he participated in the attack on the XIH Ranch . . . that he was in the room behind Uriah Gorman when Captain Hardin was killed . . . and that he participated in the attempted jailbreak."

"Is that all he said, Lieutenant?"

"No, sir. There were other things. But, sir . . . he . . . well . . . he doesn't care about this trial. He hasn't given me a chance to help him."

The cold eyes returned to Lee. They searched his face while the officer spoke. "Gorman, are you aware of the possible consequences if you are found guilty as you are charged?"

In a low tone Lee said: "I'll hang."

The captain repeated it. "You'll hang. Then why don't you try to save your life, sir?"

Lee closed his eyes. He felt dizzy from the long standing without movement. The roaring in his head lessened only when the officer's voice came more sharply.

"Do you hear me, sir?"

"Yes, I hear you."

"You will answer then."

"I don't care, Captain. I am guilty. I rode with my paw. I was there when they killed Paxton Clement and his riders. I was there when Paw killed the officer, too. I saw the whole thing. I was there at the jailhouse and, later, when Fawcett died. Later, when they caught us in the glade, I ran. I got lost in the night and just ran. I didn't have a gun any more."

"Mister Gorman, are you pleading guilty or not guilty? That's all this court is concerned with at present. Please answer."

"I told you. I'm guilty. I was there. I saw those things happen."

"Being present during the commission does not make you guilty of a crime, man!"

The captain's equanimity was slipping. His cold eyes kindled with anger. He waited with his reddening face for Lee to speak again.

The words pressed through Lee's stiff lips. "It no longer matters, sir. I can die. I guess I should die. I can't think any longer. It's . . . hard for me to stand here like this, too. I . . . I . . . ."

"Sergeant! Bring the prisoner some water."

Lee was swaying. He was a mighty oak in their midst being toppled by a terrible wind.

"Water hell, you idiot," a squat man bellowed from beyond the blue line. "Let him sit down. Fetch him a chair."

Lee remembered no more of the trial. Not even when his guard detail, trailed by Ander and Garner, craggy-faced with disapproval, returned him to the jailhouse.

Ann visited him that night. She had little to say so they sat together on the pallet touching at hip and shoulder but not looking at one another.

The second day he was taken back. It began all over again but the roaring in his mind prevented him from heeding. Ann testified. Lew Foster followed her. Others came up, were interrogated, and sent away. They were a stream of solemn faces, some ashen, some red, some filled with hate and venom.

The captain was curt. When witnesses had not seen something pertinent, he dismissed them. When they had, he listened closely. He paid particular attention to Lew Foster and the family of dead Paxton Clement. He summoned Ander and Garner, for although they had never actually seen Lee Gorman commit a crime, they could trace back the causes of the range war.

Then it was over and Lee went back to his cell. His head still hummed; voices ran together; they nagged or they were soft, or they were arrogantly demanding. He lay upon the pallet trying to lock them out. One persisted over the others. It was calling his name. A man's voice. Then it rattled the bars and he opened his eyes. The deputy U.S. marshal was there calling to him.

"Get up, boy!"

Lee struggled to his feet. He wondered if, after all, they had not finished with him. He went closer and looked stoically down into the officer's solemn face. "Yes, sir?"

"Gorman, I got something to tell you. I guess there's only one way to do it and that's straight out."

"I know," said Lee nodding. "I can guess. They're going to hang me."

237

"No, that's not it."

"It isn't . . . ?"

"No. Listen to me. They found you innocent, Gorman. Lew Foster and Ann, the Simpsons and Missus Clement . . . they said you didn't fire a shot and that you tried to help them. They aren't going to hang you. They're going to turn you loose in a day or two. But you've got to go away."

"I'll go away, Marshal."

"Dammit, I'm trying to tell you something."

"Yes, sir."

"It's about your brother Zeke."

"Yes, sir." Lee's brows drew down the slightest bit. "Zeke?"

"The soldiers found him. Him and that half-breed sheepman. They killed 'em both."

Lee's big hands closed slowly around the bars. They turned a gradual bone white. "Zeke is dead . . . ?"

The marshal inclined his head once and said roughly: "Yes. They're bringing in the bodies now. Uh . . . good night, Gorman."

Chapter Fifteen

They did not release Lee for several days and there was a good reason. Word had come—none remembered afterward who, exactly, had brought it—that Uriah Gorman had been seen southwest along the ridges near the plateau where his sheep camp had once been. Of the dozens of rumors Bob Ander and Burt Garner thought this the most plausible. For one thing it had been said that Uriah was alone. He had not been leading a savage army or hastening to attack a cow outfit. He was alone. He wasn't breathing fire and brimstone, either, or waving a clenched fist or roaring threats, but simply fading into the shadows with a furtiveness in the vicinity of his old camp. An ageing ghost in tatters, lingering in the area where he had once planned his holy war against oppression.

They discussed it. They could visualize him now returning to the place where his sweat and toil had been spent, gaunt, alone, and in wringing sadness. Where his seed had flourished, grown thick and stalwart—and had faded now into nothingness. Yes, they believed this rumor. It was in the old devil to return now.

They saddled up and left Union City before daybreak the 18th day of August, 1885. They told no one of their purpose or their destination, not even the officer or even their allies of these past searching months. They simply weighted themselves down with armament and rode quietly through the pearl-gray of coming dawn, heading southwesterly.

They rode openly as long as the misty solitude of predawn sheltered them, then, with a brightening sky overhead, they picked their way in such a manner as always to be screened by trees, sage, or bluish chaparral from the slow rising hills ahead.

By full daylight they were across the skirting stage road and into the first foothills. They rode now in single file, the deputy U.S. marshal ahead, carbine balanced across his lap and level eyes sweeping through pale light and shadows constantly. He led them quietly to the first thin ridge and did not top it, but kept on his way in such a fashion that he could see beyond while his body and the horse beneath him were still in dark shadow.

Bob Ander followed in silence. He raked the country ahead and around with long sweeps of his moving head. And he saw movement finally, blurred by both distance and the pale early light, but still movement.

"Garner, look south there. Beyond those trees to that brushy gulch where the patch of grass is."

"I see it," said the deputy U.S. marshal, drawing up. "What about it?"

"I saw movement down there."

Garner looked, saw nothing, but his heart pounded sturdily in its dark place. It would be Uriah Gorman all right. It had to be. "Let's go afoot," the deputy U.S. marshal said, and swung down, gripping his carbine. Before they moved off, doubt came and Garner strained to see better.

"It's pretty close to his old camp on that plateau," he said to Ander, hoping mightily it would be Uriah, yet doubting, too.

"Yeah, I know. With all the back country a feller wonders why he's this close. No reading a mind like that, Garner." Ander kept staring into the growing welter of soft, sad light ahead of them and below.

Burt Garner said no more but started ahead.

They skirted around the brushy slope, angling downward a little as they progressed, holding to the shadows as much as possible and making very little noise. The sun hadn't yet lighted this dark and twisted cañon, so there was no need to fear reflected light off their carbines.

Then Garner halted and straightened up slowly to peer outward and downward into the still darkened gulch. There was nothing to see, neither Uriah nor even a saddle animal. He said nothing to Ander but thought the town marshal could have seen a hundred things. A skulking coyote, a browsing deer, a bear even, or a spinner wolf.

Ander understood and spoke softly. "It was man-high. I saw that much."

Still in silence Garner pushed forward again. He did not stop until they were within a hundred yards of the grassy place, and then he only hesitated, making motions for caution, before covering another two or three hundred feet.

A watery grayness enveloped the cañon. Daylight was gradually slipping down mountain sides to dilute it. Garner got down on his belly and peered around a thick-butted old sage bush, scraggly and infernally thorned. He saw nothing. There was only a stillness as deep as death. The marshal's disappointment was strong enough to blunt his spirit. It showed in his eyes and along the sweep of his rippling jaw. He said to himself: *Let him be here. God dammit, let him be here!*

And he was.

Over a spiny distant rim the sunlight burst suddenly and showed a head-hung, tucked-up horse half hidden in the chaparral up one of the watershed little cañons beyond the glade. Ander touched him lightly. Garner ignored it. His pagan prayer had been answered and his heart was echoing like a struck anvil. He licked dry lips, pushed his carbine around the sage root, and waited. Somewhere beyond was Uriah Gorman. Ander inched closer and pressed his lips to Garner's ear.

"Mebbe he seen us or heard us."

Maybe he had, but one thing was gut sure. The old devil wouldn't get very far afoot, and the first move he made toward that horse would be his last.

Garner sweated. The wait was long, the tension great, and when he thought he could stand it no longer, a shadow glided across the open place— and Burt Garner wasn't ready.

As quickly as he dropped his head and snugged back the carbine, the raw-boned old wraith was swifter. He faded into the brush by the horse before a shot could be fired.

A thick vein at Garner's temple swelled and throbbed. His vision blurred and he stifled with great effort the violent curses in his throat.

Then Bob Ander's carbine snaked suddenly forward and grew stonestill. Garner was squinting to see Ander's target when the gun exploded beside him with a spanking echo. He heard Ander's groan through a ringing in his head.

"Missed. God dammit I missed!"

There was no answer to that. Sweat burst out over Garner. His armpits grew dark with it and his shoulders twitched. Over in the brush there was absolute stillness. Only the horse moved, turned its head to look in their direction with nervous ears.

"Did you see him good?" Garner asked.

"Not real good. Just his side and one arm."

Garner continued to watch. There was a stillness to the brush around the horse. "Maybe you got him," he said, but he didn't believe Ander had. He didn't believe you could kill a man like Uriah Gorman with one bullet. He told himself to be patient, to watch and stay still as death because now Uriah knew they were watching and he, too, had a gun.

Time dragged. The gulch turned warm, then hot, and finally Bob Ander said in a tight way: "Listen, the old cuss might be slipping around behind us. If he gets up the hillside, he can pot shoot us from up there."

Garner squirmed around for a searching look above them.

Ander said: "Maybe he'll surrender."

Garner twisted back flat and grunted. "About as likely as the Second Coming," he muttered.

"We ought to take him back alive if we can."

Garner bent a long look at the town marshal.

"Well," Ander spoke quickly, "folks're entitled to one hanging. Lord knows they've gone through enough."

Garner's reply sounded irritable. "You stick your head out there if you want, and I'll try to wing him for you. But me . . . no, sir. I came here to get him and I prefer him dead. I don't trust that crazy old bastard . . . not one damned bit I don't."

"Well, try anyway. Call out to him," Ander persisted. "Give him a chance to surrender."

Garner considered this. He did not feel, as Ander felt, that a live capture would be personal triumph. For one thing Garner did not run for office like Bob Ander; he felt differently about Uriah. He had run to earth other devils as dangerous as rattlers, and he usually brought them back dead. Now he nodded and settled his head low over the carbine.

"All right. We'll give him a chance to give up. But you watch, Ander, and if you get another glimpse, don't waste it. Kill him."

Garner called then, his voice muffled a little by the gunstock. "Hey, Gorman! We're peace officers. You going to give up peaceable or not?"

Deep silence closed in more solidly than ever. Only the horse moved slightly, stamping its feet. Ander said in puzzlement: "Maybe I did get him, after all."

Garner's squint didn't lessen. His lips barely moved when he said: "I know a good way for you to find out. Stand up where he can see you."

Ander said no more.

Then they heard it. A faint, harsh voice speaking as though the face was pressed flat against the earth, the mouth muffled by dust and dirt.

"Come and get me. I don't surrender."

Ander's excited words interrupted the marshal's dawning belief. "I *did* get him, Garner. He's hit bad, too, I can tell. He's belly down over there."

Ander got slowly upright until he could see over the sage toward the horse. No lancing flash of flame came but the silence grew thicker. Below, Burt Garner heard the deep sweep of Ander's indrawn breath, watched him move cat-footedly away from the cover toward sun-bathed thick grass. Ander was coming out of his crouch. He still held the carbine across his body with both hands, but now there was triumph and confidence across his face. Closer he went, toward the horse and the thicket where it waited.

Burt Garner gathered his weight and pushed upward onto one knee. He was breathing very shallowly. A finger slippery with sweat rested fully upon the tang of his carbine's trigger. His mouth was dry and he was very thirsty.

From ahead and to Garner's left came a single smashing roar, a great bursting flashing flame that diminished to a point. Echoes danced outward and upward through the yellow sunlight.

Bob Ander's arms flexed, flung outward casting the carbine away. Where it struck stone the gun exploded sending up a long bullet furrow of dust. He took a drunken step and lowered his head. He continued to stand there for a very long time. To Burt Garner, flat again upon the ground, it seemed that he hung like that for hours. Then he went slowly forward, face down, and pushed himself out along flatly for the full distance of his body. He did not twitch or move again.

A stringy gaunt specter appeared suddenly out of the brush. Garner saw, and forgot to fire. He stared.

Gorman's hair was matted and his speckled beard jutted wildly around a spittle-caked mouth. He strode purposefully toward the body of Town Marshal Bob Ander with his rifle wrong-ended, held over one shoulder like a club. His cheeks were so sunken the bones showed through and there was a whiteness to his green eyes. They bulged with full madness.

"Oh, you filth," he roared at the dead man. "You murdering, killing filth." He wrenched up his shoulders and swung.

Garner heard the rifle stock smash against inert flesh. It made him a little sick to the stomach.

Uriah clubbed Ander again and again, then he stopped and leaned upon the shattered rifle, sucking in the air that seemed too thin. There was a whirling before his eyes but Garner could not know that. Uriah continued to gulp air. A big old Dragoon pistol was jammed into his waistband.

Garner went lower, raised his carbine, and pinched his eyes closed to clear them of stinging sweat.

It was as though a sense had warned Gorman. He sprung upright suddenly, looking around, looking straight at Garner's hiding place. He flung the useless rifle at Garner and spun away, jerking at the belt gun as he staggered toward cover. There was glistening blood at Uriah's lower right side.

Garner fired.

Uriah was in front of the brush then. He fell into it. Hung there, a spidery skeleton in rags impaled upon the thorns and wagging its head. Garner levered up another shot. Uriah heard it. He fought loose and turned to fire. He was sinking low when the gun in his fist went off.

Garner winced at the tongue of orange flame and missed his second try. Then, in that sudden second between their shots he could hear the rattling pull of Gorman's tortured breathing and could see his grimacing face with its freshet of blood at the lips and thought detachedly his first shot had pierced the old devil's lungs. Garner fired his third and final shot.

Uriah let off a great pealing roar. He dropped the pistol and both arms hung uselessly at his sides, but he did not fall—the brush was holding him somewhat. He roared again.

It sounded to quaking Burt Garner like the scream of a panther or a lion's kill cry. He got up very slowly and moved out into the open. Uriah's head was sagging now. Garner could not see where the last slug had struck. There was blood on the old man's side and spreading in slow stain upon his shirt front. That was all. He went closer and stopped. Uriah's lips were moving slightly. Suddenly the brush snapped and Uriah fell against the earth with a rattling sound.

Garner kneeled, rolled him face up, and straightened his arms. Then he saw where the last shot had gone—through the old devil just below the belt buckle. It had broken his back. He took off his hat and held it before Uriah's face to keep out that blazing sunlight. "Gorman, can you hear me? Can you see me?"

Silence. Uriah's chest was barely rising and falling. His lips had ceased to move and his face had turned oddly peaceful. Garner placed the hat gently over his face and stood up. He made a cigarette, his fingers shaking badly. He lit it and sucked back smoke in a loud and greedy sweep of breath. Fifty feet southward Bob Ander lay in the shimmering heat, face down. The world teetered a little in his vision. He closed his eyes tightly, then sprang them wide open. The world was back as it should be again. He gazed steadily at Ander. What a god-damned fool he had been. What an idiot. You only got one chance to find out about madmen like old Gorman.

Ander's fine shining scaffold would stand empty now. All those eager breathless people back in Union City would be disappointed.

Garner inhaled deeply, flung his head to rid himself of sour sweat—and smiled. For what? For fifty thousand acres of summer-hard nothing!

He began to feel light-headed and stooped to retrieve his hat. Beneath it Uriah's face was still and serene. He experienced a slight shock. He had felt certain those eyes would be a weathered, faded steely blue. But they were green. By God the old devil had had green eyes.

He went after their horses.

Union City was quiet when Deputy U.S. Marshal Garner returned with two dead men tied to their ambling mounts. But it was uncanny how swiftly eyes saw; how swiftly word spread. He had scarcely dismounted at the livery barn when the crowd began to form. He told them nothing and went with the sergeant to the hotel where Captain Spannaus was waiting. He told everything exactly as it had happened and felt the officer's crushing stare on his face.

"Why didn't you report this before you went out, Marshal?"

"Well, because we weren't sure there was anything to it. It was just another rumor."

There was a moment of silence, then two icy words dropped into the stillness: "I see."

The marshal spoke again, his voice gathering strength and his eyes rising to hold to the officer's ascetic, fiercely mustached face. "My work is done here, Captain. I'll be leaving in the morning."

The officer appeared not to have heard. He was looking at the man who had brought Garner to him.

"Sergeant, get the Foster woman. Bring her here."

Garner left. Captain Spannaus got up, went to a window, and looked out into the dark roadway. He was thinking of Lee Gorman and how the people had reacted to his acquittal. *God,* he said to himself, *I'm sick of this. I'm so sick of Union City I could throw up!*

"Sir?"

He turned and went back to the desk without fully seeing the girl. "All right, Sergeant. That will be all. Wait outside. Madam . . . that chair there."

Ann sat. He looked at her finally, his thoughts still following their gray meanderings.

Handsome. A fine bosom . . . a good face. A man could build his life around a woman like this.

He spoke around the maze of tiredness that held him. "What are your plans now, madam?"

"Plans . . . ?"

His voice sharpened. "Yes. Your plans. You love this Gorman, don't you?"

"Yes . . ." Her tone was dull.

"And you know he has been ordered to leave this area?"

A nod.

"Then . . . what are your plans?"

"We haven't really made any . . . yet."

The captain closed his eyes, then opened them. "Are you going to leave with him?"

"Yes."

"Fine. Now, do either of you have a wagon and a team?"

"No . . . I don't think we do. The cowmen burned his wagon . . ." Ann looked up. "I suppose I can get one from my paw."

"Is he still in town?"

"Yes."

"Then go ask him. If he gives you one, have it back here in front of the hotel by sunup. Do you understand?"

Ann said—"Yes."—again, and stood up.

The captain remained seated but he nodded to indicate dismissal. Then he watched her cross to the door and pass beyond.

"Sergeant . . . ?"

"Yes, sir!"

"How are the townsmen taking it . . . about Ander?"

"Not very well, sir."

"I see. Well, relay my orders to Lieutenants Bertram and Meade that the column pulls out at sunup for Fort Laramie."

"Yes, sir!"

"And one more thing, Sergeant. See that the Foster woman and Gorman go with us. We'll act as an escort at least as far as Hatchersville. That ought to be far enough to get them started on their way. Clear?"

"Yes, sir!"

About the Author

Lauran Paine who, under his own name and various pseudonyms has written over a thousand books, was born in Duluth, Minnesota. His family moved to California when he was at a young age and his apprenticeship as a Western writer came about through the years he spent in the livestock trade, rodeos, and even motion pictures where he served as an extra because of his expert horsemanship in several films starring movie cowboy Johnny Mack Brown. In the late 1930s, Paine trapped wild horses in northern Arizona and even, for a time, worked as a professional farrier. Paine came to know the Old West through the eyes of many who had been born in the previous century, and he learned that Western life had been very different from the way it was portrayed on the screen. "I knew men who had killed other men," he later recalled. "But they were the exceptions. Prior to and during the Depression, people were just too busy eking out an existence to indulge in Saturday-night brawls." He served in the U.S. Navy in the Second World War and began writing for Western pulp magazines following his discharge. It is interesting to note that all of his earliest novels (written under his own name and the pseudonym Mark Carrel) were published in the British market and he soon had as strong a following in that country as in the United States. Paine's Western fiction is characterized by strong plots, authenticity, an apparently effortless ability to construct situation and character, and a preference for building his stories upon a solid foundation of historical fact. *Adobe Empire* (1956), one of his best novels, is a fictionalized account of the last twenty years in the life of trader William Bent and, in an off-trail way, has a melancholy, bittersweet texture that is not easily forgotten. In later novels like *The White Bird* (1997) and *Cache Cañon* (1998), he showed that the special magic and power of his stories and characters had only matured along with his basic themes of changing times, changing attitudes, learning from experience, respecting Nature, and the yearning for a simpler, more moderate way of life.

Center Point Large Print
600 Brooks Road / PO Box 1
Thorndike ME 04986-0001 USA

(207) 568-3717

US & Canada:
1 800 929-9108
www.centerpointlargeprint.com

.

GAYLORD

MN